Bagthorpes Besieged

Helen Cresswell was born in Nottinghamshire and educated at Nottingham Girls' High School and King's College, London, where she took a degree in English. She now lives in a village in north Nottinghamshire and has two daughters. She has been writing from the age of seven, and is the author of many popular children's books, including *The Piemakers, Dear Shrink, and The Secret World of Polly Flint.* This is her ninth novel in the hilarious *Bagthorpe Saga.*

by the same author

The Bagthorpe Saga (in order of publication)
Ordinary Jack
Absolute Zero
Bagthorpes Unlimited
Bagthorpes v The World
Bagthorpes Abroad
Bagthorpes Haunted
Bagthorpes Liberated
The Bagthorpe Triangle
***
Moondial
The Secret World of Polly Flint
Dear Shrink
The Winter of the Birds
The Bongleweed
The Piemakers
The Signposters
The Night-Watchmen
The Beachcombers
The Outlanders
Up the Pier
Where the Wind Blows

BAGTHORPES BESIEGED

being the ninth part of the Bagthorpe Saga

Helen Cresswell

faber and faber

First published in 1996
This paperback edition published 1997
by Faber and Faber Limited
3 Queen Square London WC1N 3AU

Photoset by Parker Typesetting Service, Leicester
Printed and bound in Great Britain by Mackays of Chatham PLC, Chatham, Kent

A CIP record for this book is available from the British Library
ISBN 0–571–17948–7

10 9 8 7 6 5 4 3

One

The Bagthorpes were out of the Triangle but still in the woods. In the last volume of their exploits people were coming and going as never before. There was as much coming and going, and as many cases of mistaken identities, as in *A Midsummer Night's Dream* – and some.

Let us recapitulate.

1 Mrs Bagthorpe uttered a Primal Scream and went missing from Unicorn House, and is currently at eleven Coldharbour Road with Mrs Fosdyke and her son Max.

2 Mr Bagthorpe was arrested for not knowing his car's make and number, and knocking off a police officer's cap. He has just been released after a neat blackmailing job by Uncle Parker.

3 The whisky-swigging tramp Mr O'Toole, having been suspected of being a terrorist or a serial killer, or both, was arrested and put in the cell next to Mr Bagthorpe's. He has just been released following a neat blackmailing job by Uncle Parker.

4 Aunt Celia is expecting Phantom Twins. (This is a condition not known to medical science, but she has it anyway.)

5 Mrs Fosdyke has muddied already murky waters for the police by wrongly identifying her own son as (a) The Knaresborough Knifer and (b) a terrorist bomber.

6 Her son Max, while being neither of the above, is on the run from the police having fraudulently used a stolen cash card. He has turned up after a ten-year absence.

7   Daisy Parker, having recently alienated Grandma's clair-
voyante by monkeying with her tarot cards and smashing her
goldfish bowl, is now in a Quiet Phase. This, as followers of the
Saga will know, is ominous. It is the calm before the storm, the
creak of ice before the *Titanic* hits the iceberg.
8   Billy Goat Gruff has destroyed the nursery at The Knoll,
and laid waste Aunt Celia's bower, both within hours. This is
his all-time record (to date). He is with his owner, at Unicorn
House. So, for all we know, is Arry Awk.

When last seen, Uncle Parker, Mr Bagthorpe, Jack and Mr
O'Toole were wedged in a taxi after leaving Aysham Police
Station by the back door. (The front entrance was besieged by
the media, under the mistaken impression that the Knaresborough Knifer was in there. By the kerb was Uncle Parker's
scarlet roadster, nobly abandoned by him in order to make good
their getaway. This was to turn out to be the only ray of
sunshine in the police's day.)

The quartet in the cab travelled in silence for the most part.
Uncle Parker did attempt the odd quip, on the lines of 'Well,
Henry, so now you've got a police record. So had Oscar Wilde,
of course, and Bertrand Russell. All grist to the mill.'

Mr Bagthorpe did not respond because his teeth were too
tightly clenched. There are few more mortifying experiences
than being bailed out by a lifelong adversary. Later, Mr
Bagthorpe would claim that he had *wanted* to be in police
custody, that it was research for his latest script. His first real
chance to enter the mind of a wrongfully arrested person had
now been blown by Uncle Parker's busybodying intervention.
He would even threaten to sue.

Mr O'Toole was silent because he was in his customary fog.
It was some twenty hours since he had had his last tot of
Scotch, but he had in no way dried out. He was probably in
much the same state of consciousness as Aunt Celia was for

much of the time, the difference being that she used meditation, stretchy dancing and goldfish-watching to achieve it. Mr O'Toole took a short cut via the bottle – usually paid for by someone else.

The other three, however, might have been silent, but were all thinking, not to say plotting. Let us share their thoughts, which were roughly along the following lines:

Jack: Uncle Park's brilliant, he's a bigger genius than all us Bagthorpes put together. He got Father and Mr O'Toole out of jug and never even paid a penny bail. That policeman's face! Mind you, Father's not going to like it. I wonder what he's done with the Hoover and the sucked-up sock? And the car? When we get home, at least we'll find out what's been going on – all that stuff with Fozzy on the telly. All that stuff about terrorists and bombs. And perhaps Mother'll have turned up. Just because the police wanted her dental records it doesn't necessarily mean she's dead. She's not dead, she's not!

Uncle Parker: Poor old Henry. Going to take some living down, this little lot. Not over yet, either. That bunch of paparazzi outside the station isn't going to let this one go. They'll be on his tracks, sure as eggs. I hope to God those half-baked police keep an eye on my car. Still, at least I've got O'Toole. That'll perk Celia up no end. Mind you, he doesn't look much of a guru without that frock. Looks more or less what he is – a stinking tramp. The main thing is to make sure he ends up at our place. Should be a doddle. Just let Henry and young Jack get out, then tell the driver to drive on. Simple. Poor old Jack, having to live with that bunch.

Bagthorpe: What have I done to deserve this? What have I ever done? I'll sue. It's wrongful arrest. Even in this benighted country you can't get done for not knowing your car's make and number. I'll get on to my MP. I'll get on to the Home Secretary. I might get compensation. It'll run into six figures. I'm a sensitive creative writer. God knows what damage will have been done – I might not be able to write another script for weeks. Months. Years. I might never write another word. It'll run into millions.

And Russell can wipe that smirk off his face. He still owes me for my curdled pond and all those dead goldfish. Why are we in a taxi? Where's his car? Wrapped round a tree, I hope. Why don't the police arrest *him*? Gin-swigging tailor's dummy! And what's that filthy tramp doing here? He's not coming back to my place, that's for sure. Did those mutton-headed police run a test on him while they'd got him? Blood pure alcohol, I shouldn't wonder. One hundred per cent proof. Pity I can't sue him. God, I could use a drink.

These, then, were their thoughts. What the taxi-driver was thinking is not known.

When the car drew up in front of Unicorn House, Mr Bagthorpe wrenched open the door and climbed out.

'Jack – quick! Out!' (Another of his thoughts had been that he would make sure Uncle Parker paid off the taxi. He was, of course, playing unwittingly straight into his enemy's hands.)

Jack climbed out.

'Drive on!' ordered Uncle Parker. His abduction of Mr O'Toole was even easier than he had contemplated.

Jack stood uncertainly in the drive, gazing at his home. It seemed light-years since he had last seen it.

'Come on,' he said, 'let's see if Mother's back.'

Whether his wife was still missing was neither here nor there to Mr Bagthorpe. He was striding towards the house congratulating himself on avoiding a taxi fare and ridding himself of the tramp at a single stroke. Jack hurried after him.

The house was uncannily silent. Grandma's cracked Valkyries were not playing because her son was not there to be driven mad

4

by them. Even so, Jack thought, one would have expected to hear something. His siblings were not noted for silence, and given that Billy Goat Gruff was in the house, one would at least have expected to hear the sound of him chewing something, or otherwise destroying it.

Mr Bagthorpe flung open the kitchen door. He and Jack were greeted by the smell of a burned fry-up and a simultaneous explosion of breath, followed by a chorus of accusations. William, Tess and Rosie glared at their father, whom they had written off as detained indefinitely in a police cell.

'*Now* look what you've done!'

'I could've lasted hours yet!'

'I was going for a record!'

The trio, Jack noted with interest, had unusually red faces. These could not have been blushes. The Bagthorpes, with the exception of Jack himself, never blushed. On the table before them was a stop-watch and a piece of paper that looked like some kind of score card. That figured. For the young Bagthorpes, competition was the name of the game. Life itself, so far as they were concerned, was one long competition.

'We'll have to start again,' William said. 'Stop the watch.'

'What're you doing?' Jack asked.

'Seeing who can hold their breath longest,' replied Rosie. 'And I was winning, and you would go and ruin it!'

'As far as I'm concerned, the whole lot of you can hold your breath till kingdom come,' their father told them.

'What're you doing out of prison?' demanded Rosie. 'I thought you were supposed to be in prison.'

'You didn't really clock a policeman, did you, Father?' asked William.

'Your father in prison under wrongful arrest, and all you lot can do is sit round holding your breath!' Mr Bagthorpe was disgusted. In so far as he had bothered imagining how his family might feel about this, he had imagined them as distraught. 'Has anyone got on to my MP? Has anyone contacted the Home Secretary?'

'Who *is* your MP, Father?' inquired Tess. She knew that he did not know, and he knew that she knew he did not.

'And who's the Home Secretary?' William followed up the advantage.

'The way this government is everlastingly shuffling it could be anyone. Here today, gone tomorrow.' Mr Bagthorpe was blustering. 'Use your initiative. Ring Directory Enquiries. Ring Downing Street.'

'Come *on*, everybody,' said Rosie. 'Are we holding our breath or not?'

'Has Mother come back?' Jack asked.

'D'you think you two could go out while we do it?' William said. 'We can't do it with you standing there interrupting.'

Mr Bagthorpe set off in the direction of his study and cache of Scotch, and Jack followed. In the hall they stopped dead.

There, plonk in front of them, was Billy Goat Gruff. He stared meditatively at them with unwinking yellow eyes, chewing. Beneath him was a large puddle.

The trio stood locked in tableau for several seconds. Then Mr Bagthorpe let out a blood-curdling cry, dodged past the goat and made for his study. The door banged behind him. Jack heard the chink of glass as his father poured a stiff drink with trembling hands.

'Is that you, Henry?'

It was Grandma, from above, presumably still holed up there with Daisy.

'Yes, Grandma. It's us!' Jack called.

There was a brief pause. Then, at a volume that sent the goat twitching and rolling his eyes, came the hellish cacophony of the fractured Vienna State Opera Company. Mr Bagthorpe's homecoming was complete.

*

6

At number eleven Coldharbour Road a homecoming of a very different kind was being celebrated (for want of a better word). Mrs Fosdyke had only really liked her son as a baby. She was finding it hard to reconcile this dishevelled, long-haired man and her fond memories of Max in a pram, shaking his rattle. She tried hard to convince herself that this stranger was that baby. She tried to picture him in bonnet and knitted matinée coat. The effect was unnerving.

Mrs Bagthorpe, on the other hand, was finding her meeting with Max extremely therapeutic. Her threatened nervous breakdown was receding by the minute. She had a role to play – two roles, as counsellor and magistrate.

Max had confessed why he was on the run. Mrs Fosdyke, who in some confused way had almost come to believe that he was the terrorist bomber spotted earlier in the day, was relieved to find that this was not the case.

'There's never been any terrorists in my family,' she declared. This would have been news to Mr Bagthorpe. She was, however, disgusted to find that her son had been mixed up in credit cards.

'I'm surprised at you!' she told him severely. ' 'Orrible evil things! Cut mine up to mince, I did, and sent it back to the bank.'

This was true. She had done this partly to avoid having the card misappropriated by the likes of her own son.

' 'Ow did you know the number?' she demanded. 'They've all got magic numbers.'

'Told me,' he mumbled, meaning the landlady in Bridlington whose card it was.

'Did you use force, Max?' inquired Mrs Bagthorpe magisterially. 'Don't be afraid to tell the truth. Everything will be taken into consideration, including your own openness and willingness to cooperate.'

'I asked her what the number was and said if she didn't tell me I'd knock 'er bleeding block off,' Max said.

'That is certainly a threat of violence,' said Mrs Bagthorpe. 'It is certainly demanding money with menaces. You did not actually produce a knife, or a gun?'

'Oooh – gun!' moaned Mrs Fosdyke, and scooted off to put the kettle on again. Hot sweet tea was in demand as never before.

'I never!' said Max. 'All I done was this!' He raised and clenched a puny fist.

'Good,' said Mrs Bagthorpe encouragingly. 'That is certainly in your favour, Max.'

'I was desperate,' he confided. 'Starving, see.'

'That is an exonerating circumstance.' Mrs Bagthorpe, as magistrate, was certainly a soft touch. She made excuses for people that they would not have dreamed of making for themselves. 'And I expect you felt it more honourable to obtain money by whatever means, and fend for yourself, rather than throw yourself on the State. I expect it was a matter of pride and self-esteem.'

'Eh? What? Oh, yeah. Will I get sent down?'

Not as long as Mrs Bagthorpe was on the Bench.

'You did exactly the right thing in making for home,' she told him. 'I expect that, once here, you intended to find a job and pay back the money.'

'Oh, yeah,' agreed Max, who could not even remember the name and address of the landlady concerned. 'I was going to pay 'er back every penny. Even if it killed me. Wiv interest,' he added virtuously.

'That is highly commendable,' she told him. 'You have had an excellent upbringing and devoted mother, and are of previously unblemished character.'

Max had, in fact, over the years done the odd spot of purloining and fiddling, but had not so far been nicked for it.

'I expect you were overcome with remorse the moment you had obtained the fifty pounds,' Mrs Bagthorpe continued. 'Your instinct was to come home and confess all to your mother.'

Max had not had any instinct to come home during a full ten years away; the thought had not even crossed his mind. He had done so now only as a last resort, and had certainly not intended to share his feelings with his mother. Seeing her again had served only to confirm the wisdom of his leaving home in the first place. If Max had not improved over the years in Mrs Fosdyke's eyes, nor had she in his.

'That done,' Mrs Bagthorpe went on, 'all that remains is for you to go to the police and confess. After having a bath,' she added, 'and a haircut.'

She knew only too well the prejudices that exist against the hairy and the unwashed.

'The police!' Mrs Fosdyke, re-entering with her tray, nearly dropped it on the spot.

'Certainly, Mrs Fosdyke,' said Mrs Bagthorpe. 'He has nothing to fear. In fact, it will count in his favour.'

'But they think 'e's a bomber!' screeched Mrs Fosdyke. 'They're out looking for 'im! 'E'll be all over the papers!'

He would be all over the papers read by her neighbours. This, to Mrs Fosdyke, was the ultimate nightmare. Max could have throttled an old-age pensioner in his bath, for all she cared, as long as it did not get into the papers. He could have shot the Prime Minister. He could have garrotted the Queen.

'I think it most unlikely,' her employer assured her. 'The case may very well be dismissed. And he is not a bomber – a terrorist – remember.'

' 'Ow do we know they won't prove 'e is?' Mrs Fosdyke was not comforted. 'They're always doing it. Look at them Guildford Nine and Birmingham Three!'

'There will be no evidence whatever to connect him with any bomb.'

'They'll *invent* it!' Mrs Fosdyke sometimes thought her employer impossibly naïve.

9

'Nor', Mrs Bagthorpe reminded her, '*was* there a bomb, in fact. The bag thought to contain one was my own, remember. If necessary, I shall testify to that effect.'

'Well, I suppose that'd be something,' Mrs Fosdyke grudgingly conceded. 'I expect they'll listen to you. You're not a long-'aired layabout.'

Max, hearing this, could have been left in little doubt of his place in his mother's esteem.

' 'E could do with a bath, all right, *and* 'is 'air cut.'

There came a knock on the door. All three jumped.

'Quick! 'Ide!' Mrs Fosdyke ran at her son and prodded him towards the stairs. He scuttled up them to the sanctuary of his room – teddy-bears, teething rings and all.

'What if it's the police?' hissed Mrs Fosdyke.

'I shall deal with them,' replied Mrs Bagthorpe. 'Compose yourself.'

Mrs Fosdyke looked anything but composed, eyes like hatpins and hands wringing in the manner of Lady Macbeth trying to out the damned spot. The fact that the knock had come at the front door, rather than the back, was in itself unsettling. It was now repeated.

Mrs Fosdyke edged up to the door and stared into the frosted glass for clues to the identity of the caller.

' 'Oo is it?' she croaked. She would have done this anyway. Mrs Fosdyke read her own newspaper to good effect, and was not in the habit of opening her door to uninvited callers.

'Mrs Fosdyke?' came a woman's voice.

'What if it is?' replied that lady noncommittally.

'If we could just have a word?'

'Is it the police?'

'No. We're sorry to disturb you like this, but you don't seem to be on the phone.'

'I don't believe in 'em,' said Mrs Fosdyke flatly.

This was mainly because she had the unbudgeable conviction

10

that subscribers were charged for incoming, as well as out-going, calls. She was not, she declared, going to pay hundreds of pounds for every Tom, Dick or Harry to go ringing her up at all hours of the day and night. Also, of course, phones were bugged.

'It was just a short interview we were after, Mrs Fosdyke.'

Mrs Fosdyke looked nervously up the stairs. She licked her lips.

'About your resourcefulness and bravery in dealing with the Knaresborough Knifer and the terrorist.'

Nobody had ever called Mrs Bagthorpe resourceful before, or brave. That description had certainly never been splashed all over the papers for the whole world to read.

'I should think very carefully about it, Mrs Fosdyke,' called Mrs Bagthorpe from the living-room. 'Publicity and fame can be great destroyers of lives.'

If she had had her wits about her, she would have noticed that a man at the window was already operating a camera, and her own publicity and fame were already in the bag.

'We shall be happy to pay you, of course,' came the voice through the letter-box.

'Oooh!' exclaimed Mrs Fosdyke unguardedly. She had read of the huge sums paid out for newspaper stories. She should, of course, have kept her cool. She should have replied that that depended on how *much* money. She should have negotiated, kept adding noughts. Better still, she should have picked up her phone (had she had one) and got herself an agent.

'A substantial sum,' said the voice. 'Our readers will love it. They're always interested in ordinary people rising to the heights of heroism.'

The reporter could already see a possible headline:

FEARLESS FOZZY FOILS FIEND

So could Mrs Fosdyke. She was already shooting back bolts,

turning the key. Some old wary instinct made her open the door still on the chain, and peer through the aperture. (For all she knew, the Knaresborough Knifer was an adept female impersonator.) What she saw reassured her. She undid the chain.

'Good evening, Mrs Fosdyke!' The reporter was through the door in a flash. In the past, she had even shouldered and kicked chained doors, and been in in a flash. 'Patsy Page of the *Sludge*. Come on, Gary!'

'Oooh!' Mrs Fosdyke was enchanted. She was not familiar with the name, but this was her very own paper, her daily Bible. 'Ever so pleased to meet you!'

She led the way into her living-room. The photographer was already at work, capturing Mrs Fosdyke against her cabbage-rose wallpaper, and, for good measure, Mrs Bagthorpe, who sat with knitted brow.

Her brow had knitted when she heard the identity of the newspaper. She did not, however, rise and forbid the taking of her photograph, as she would have done under normal circumstances. Mrs Bagthorpe was not yet herself. She had merely moved from a generalized obsession with getting away from the world, to a specific obsession with saving and reforming Max. She had tunnel vision.

'What about a nice cup of 'ot sweet tea?' suggested Mrs Fosdyke, more or less automatically.

'Oh, I think we can do better than that, Mrs Fosdyke,' said Patsy Page. She dug into her voluminous bag and produced the brandy she always carried. This was partly to keep herself warm during long vigils outside people's houses, and partly as an aid to loosening the tongues of interviewees.

Mrs Fosdyke trotted off to fetch glasses.

'There's really no phone?' asked Ms Page. 'Jeez!'

She produced a portable one and tapped out a number. Mrs Fosdyke reappeared just as she was concluding her call.

'Oooh, is that one of them moving phones?'

'Mobile. Yeah. Right, everyone – cheers!' She downed her brandy in one gulp, and Mrs Fosdyke unwisely followed suit.

'Now . . . where exactly was this bomb . . . and tell me your feelings when you first saw this man . . . as much detail as you can remember, please . . .'

With these harmless words the meteoric rise to stardom of Mrs Fosdyke began.

Two

As the taxi journeyed on towards The Knoll, Uncle Parker remembered Jack's earlier words about the frock. A voluminous purple and gold affair, this has been Mrs Bagthorpe's, but had been passed over to the tramp while his own smelly get-up was being washed. It had given this huge, bearded figure a certain air, and had convinced Aunt Celia that here was her guru, her spiritual guide.

Uncle Parker had the distinct impression that Jack had said this garment was now concealed among the laurels in his own drive.

'Stop here a mo, will you?' He tapped the driver's shoulder.

'But we ain't there yet,' he objected. In his experience, fares usually travelled to their own doors, not half-way up their drives.

'Stop!' repeated Uncle Parker.

He hopped nimbly out and started to rummage among the laurels, watched by the bemused driver.

' 'Ere!' he said to the semi-recumbent Mr O'Toole, 'This is *'is* place? 'E ain't up to something?'

During the course of the day he had heard odd snatches on his radio, concerning a terrorist bomber and the Knaresborough Knifer – both, apparently, now in the immediate vicinity. He had no wish to be run in as accomplice to either of these felons.

'Could be using me as a getaway car,' he thought. He looked

nervously through his rear-view mirror at the bearded occupant of the back seat. Mr O'Toole's eyes were closed.

'Looks as if 'e's under the influence,' the taxi-driver thought. 'Drugs probably.'

The scenario was growing hairier by the moment.

' 'Ere! You!' Mr O'Toole's eyes opened. 'What's going on? What's 'e doing in them bushes?'

Concealing a bomb, as likely as not, with trip wires. Or a body.

'Soon be home,' said the tramp dreamily. Uncle Parker had whispered this to him several times during the journey. 'It'll flow like water, so it will.'

By this he meant Scotch. Uncle Parker had also assured him of this. What sprang to the taxi-driver's mind was blood.

' 'Strewth!'

He began a frantic three-point turn. Shrubs rocked, gravel flew. Once turned, he put his foot down and raced off at a lick that Uncle Parker himself could hardly have equalled. He ducked his head as he drove, half expecting a hail of bullets to follow him.

Uncle Parker, the retrieved garment over his arm, emerged from the shrubbery to see the tail lights of his taxi disappear round a bend.

'What the . . .?' Uncle Parker was rarely thrown, but he was now. The taxi had driven off, fare unpaid, with Mr O'Toole still in the back. The whole thing was inexplicable. It was bizarre. He cast round for some possible explanation. Some momentous domestic crisis must have been relayed over the cab's intercom, he decided. House on fire? Wife giving birth to twins?

His face clouded as he remembered that his own wife was expecting a happy event of that order. The twins Aunt Celia was expecting were never likely to present a medical emergency, in that they existed only in her mind. She was experiencing, her consultant had assured him, a Phantom Pregnancy. This had been a relatively uncomplicated matter until Uncle Parker had himself complicated it by suggesting to his wife that she might even be expecting twins. With Aunt Celia, a little suggestion went a very long way. If you suggested to her that she was growing wings, she would probably take off.

'Better get after him!'

Uncle Parker started to lope up the drive towards his garage. Then he remembered. His own car was outside Aysham Police Station. There was no second car. Aunt Celia did not drive. In the early days of their marriage, he had offered to teach her, sweeping away her protests. 'Easy as falling off a log,' he had assured her.

They had got no further than the first lesson, which took place in their own drive. Each time the engine was switched on Aunt Celia had screamed. The car was alive, she had maintained, had become a malevolent entity with a will of its own.

'Switch it off, switch it off!' she had screamed.

In the end she had got out and run back into the house, hands over her ears. It was weeks before Uncle Parker had managed to coax her to get back into the car, even with himself at the wheel. (This in itself was not surprising. Few people willingly got into Uncle Parker's car with him at the wheel.)

In many ways it was a mercy that Aunt Celia had never passed her driving test. This would have involved a familiarity with the Highway Code, an elementary grasp of speed limits, and the significance of signs reading SLOW, or REDUCE SPEED NOW. As it was, she was perfectly happy to sit at her husband's side as he blithely ignored these signs, though on these occasions he did make an effort to reduce the frequency of Emergency Stops.

Uncle Parker was now at a loss. He had set his heart on delivering the tramp to his wife and seeing her face light up.

16

She was there alone in the house, with her destroyed bower and nursery. He remembered the gynaecologist's words: 'It is important', he had said, 'to avoid any shock to the nervous system. We must proceed with caution.'

Uncle Parker looked thoughtfully down at the garment over his arm. He was of the opinion that it was wearing this that had given Mr O'Toole the misleading appearance of a spiritual master.

'That, and the beard,' he thought. 'Can't do much about the beard, but . . .'

The idea he now had was appealing. What if he himself were to wear the frock? If Celia accepted him as guru, endowed with ancient wisdom, it would kill several birds with one stone. First, it would relieve him of the necessity to look for the tramp. Uncle Parker had no idea where the taxi-driver was taking him. It might even be back to the police station. Second, he had no real wish to entertain that gentleman as indefinite house guest. He had enough on his plate with Daisy and Billy Goat Gruff (though admittedly this pair did not make drastic inroads into his stock of malt). Third, he knew that his wife must sooner or later be told that the twins she was expecting were Phantoms. It would be easier for him to tell her this if he were a guru. He could put a mystical gloss on the thing, make it seem as if it were destined. (Aunt Celia went great guns on Destiny.)

All in all, the experiment seemed worth trying. Uncle Parker let himself quietly into the house and tiptoed upstairs. There he set about the transformation. He removed his suit and pulled the frock over his head. He then, with some misgivings, regarded himself in the full-length mirror.

Mrs Bagthorpe was shorter than either himself or the tramp, but had bought the garment for evenings, and had been pregnant with Rosie at the time. It was, therefore, quite a decent length, while not concealing his shoes and socks. These looked distinctly un-Maharishi-like. He accordingly removed them, and decided that he would make his first appearance to his wife barefoot. He was pleased with this idea, having a vague impression that a lot of toddling around barefoot went on in India.

'They're always doing it,' he thought. 'And walking on coals, and sleeping on beds of nails, and so forth.'

He had no ambitions to do either of these last, and very much hoped Aunt Celia would not have heard about them. (He would probably have had a stab at both, if pushed. His unaccountable besottedness with his spouse was legendary.)

He studied his reflection. He tried to see himself as he would appear to his wife's eyes. He was himself deeply unhappy with his image. He was a snappy dresser, and by no means conventional, but had never so far worn a frock.

'Not my style.'

Further touches were necessary, he felt. He rummaged among Aunt Celia's jewellery, and came up with a decently ethnic-looking string of beads. He added a bangle. And another. He decorated himself with the same thoroughness as his daughter decorated Billy Goat Gruff. It was lucky that Rosie was not there to photograph him.

Finally, he practised looking wise and all-knowing. This was not easy. He tried hard to imagine how Gielgud would go about it.

'Need some more props,' he decided, and quietly descended the stairs.

The first of these props was a stiff gin and tonic. The second, he decided, should be music. Something to set the mood, something cosmic and ethereal. There was plenty of this about. Uncle Parker selected a disc and switched on the stereo. He flicked on the speakers all about the house. Music flooded it.

As he went through the hall his glance rested on one of the knights in armour, sword buckled at his side. An inspiration struck him. He unfastened the sword and raised it aloft.

'The sword of truth!' he told himself. 'She'll like that. The sword of truth, cutting through the darkness of the universe!'

He gave his frock a final twitch, assumed what he hoped was an all-seeing, all-knowing expression, and padded towards the sitting-room.

As he approached, he became aware that mingled with the music were strange wails. They rose and fell on a high, eerie note. Uncle Parker had never heard quite such a sound before, never having been present at any wake where keening went on. Aunt Celia, who went in for moaning and screaming on a regular basis, had certainly never before done this kind of rhythmic, almost hypnotic wailing.

He cautiously pushed open the sitting-room door and peered in. Aunt Celia was on her knees, her arms uplifted as if in supplication, here eyes closed. She swayed as she wailed.

Uncle Parker was well and truly foxed. Had he thought the thing through, he might have decided that the introduction of music was not a wise move. Aunt Celia believed herself to be alone in the house. She had not heard the tyres on gravel that would usually herald her husband's approach, and he had let himself in quietly and tiptoed upstairs. Given this, spontaneously erupting music must have given her a very nasty shock.

Any normal person would have thought that a music-loving burglar was on the premises, and run for the poker. To Aunt Celia, there was only one explanation. The music was a kind of visitation, emanating from a supernatural source. It probably heralded an angel, she thought, given that she was to give birth to mystical twins. She accordingly fell to her knees and wailed in ecstasy.

Just as Uncle Parker poked his head round the door she peeped through her eyelashes for signs of any manifestation. There was (naturally) no sign of any angel. She therefore decided to give it some encouragement. She ceased her wailing, and chanted invocations instead.

'I am ready, ready! Come, I am prepared!'

Uncle Parker still did not grasp what was going on. It was, however, clearly something of a mystical order, and, as such, conducive to his appearance as a barefoot guru. He advanced toward her.

'Speak, I am listening! Come to me, I am prepared!'

At this point she opened her eyes. Aunt Celia was expecting an angel – possibly two of them – haloed in light. What she saw was her own husband in a hideous purple and orange frock, dripping bangles and beads and brandishing a sword. The gap between expectation and reality was awesome.

The shock was too much for her delicate nervous system – it would have been too much for almost anybody's. She uttered a low cry and fainted clean away.

Uncle Parker was well used to fielding his wife's fainting form, but on this occasion could not reach her in time. Fortunately, she had fallen from a kneeling position and on to a deep pile carpet. He dropped his sword and ran and knelt beside her, cradling her in his arms.

'Celia, dearest, it's me. Celia!'

At this moment there came a knock on the front door. It was an urgent kind of knocking, rather than that of people who come round selling dishcloths at two pounds each, or offering to tell you about Jesus.

Uncle Parker hesitated, then gently lowered his wife and hurried to the door. He flung it open.

'Good grief!' he exclaimed, disgusted.

The two policemen stood there. He stared at them and they stared back. All in all, they had more to stare about. They, after all, were wearing perfectly ordinary regulation uniform. They had come to investigate a report of a man acting suspiciously in the bushes after having hijacked a taxi. (The driver, naturally, had touched his story up a little.) They had assumed this to be the terrorist sighted earlier in Coldharbour Road. (The Bomb

Squad had been called there, but found no bomb. The police still insisted that the man was a terrorist. It was a matter of saving face.)

The police were now baffled. No IRA bomber they had heard of had ever gone round in a frock wearing women's jewellery.

' 'Er – fancy dress, is it?' said one.

Uncle Parker, who had no time at all for the police, rudely turned his back on them and hurried back to tend his wife. The officers, exchanging a glance and a nod, ran after him and into the sitting-room, where an unconscious female lay on the floor. Near by lay a large, deadly looking sword. Music was coming from everywhere, no doubt to drown her screams.

Uncle Parker was on his knees beside the prostrate figure.

'Celia! Forgive me, dearest! I didn't mean to . . .'

The senior officer fished out his radio.

'Murder. The Knoll, Passingham. Repeat – murder.'

Meanwhile, at number eleven Coldharbour Road, Mrs Fosdyke was in her element. Never before had she been photographed so many times, never before had someone hung upon her every word and written it down in a notebook.

Patsy Page was in a state of considerable bemusement. Despite every effort to keep Mrs Fosdyke to the point, her narrative was littered with references to dead goldfish, refrigerated knitting and Billy goats. There was also a lot about someone called Daisy, and about sucked-up socks.

'There isn't just one story here,' she thought, 'there are several. We could run and run. And as for the old bat – what a find! Could be another Eddie the Eagle.'

She decided to file her story, then quiz Mrs Fosdyke further the next day. She poured everyone another generous slug of brandy and took out her mobile phone.

'Is there somewhere quiet I can go to ring through?' she asked. 'It's an Exclusive.'

'You could go up – ' Mrs Fosdyke started, then stopped. Max was upstairs, on the run from the police.

'In the kitchen,' she said. 'It's lovely and quiet in there.'

The reporter went off. The other three sat and looked at one another.

'Isn't it exciting?' said Mrs Fosdyke.

The photographer, who was used to training telephoto lenses on unwary celebrities, was not the least bit excited. Nor was he pleased with the pictures he had taken. He considered Mrs Fosdyke to be supremely unphotogenic.

Mrs Bagthorpe's mind was on Max, on his reform and rehabilitation. She had hardly heard a word Mrs Fosdyke had said to the reporter. This was just as well, given that it contained numerous slanderous references to her own family.

'I'm afraid I don't feel at all excited, Mrs Fosdyke,' she said. 'In fact, I don't feel anything at all, really.'

'That'll be the reaction, Mrs Bagthorpe dear,' said Mrs Fosdyke wisely. 'After all the excitement. There's always calm after the storm. Isn't there?' She appealed to the photographer.

He was not prepared to enter into a discussion about the nature of excitement. He grunted.

'I should doubt if I'll sleep a wink tonight, after this,' she continued. (She probably would, after the quantity of brandy she had consumed.) 'I 'ave trouble sleeping, you know.'

She addressed the photographer rather than her employer, who was already well aware of her ongoing battle with insomnia. She launched into an account of its pattern, and the various means she employed to combat it.

'It don't do to take them capsules,' she said. 'Oh no. First step to ruination, that is. There's people all over everywhere going round 'alf drugged and suing their doctors, my paper says. And once they're on 'em, they can't get off. 'Abituated, see. Slave to an 'abit. You won't catch me getting slave to an 'abit.'

This, coming from Mrs Fosdyke, was rich. She was governed

22

by habit from the moment she woke and pushed her feet straight into the fur-edged slippers that kept off the cramps, to the moment she went to bed, having checked all her defences against murderers and rapists in immutable order. She always poured the milk before the tea, used exactly sixty strokes when brushing her teeth, and said 'Bless you!' every time someone sneezed (even when Mr Bagthorpe had hay fever). Her whole life ran on rails, and was rather more predictable than a British Rail timetable.

'I'll take pills along with anybody,' she declared, 'but not for sleeping. Oh no.'

She then went on to detail her own strategies for wooing sleep. 'A nice 'ot milky drink,' she advised. 'Cocoa, or 'Orlicks, or such. Ever so good for the nerves. And a nice 'ot-water bottle.'

Once one of these much-used items had leaked in Mrs Fosdyke's bed, and Mrs Bagthorpe had offered her an electric blanket. She had reacted strongly against this.

'There's people die every night from one of them,' she asserted. 'Electrification. They find 'em in the morning and their eyes is all staring, with the shock, see. And they give off invisible rays that get in your bones while you're asleep, and give you 'orrible diseases. You're not telling me that a bit of rubber and 'ot water can give you a 'orrible disease.'

Mrs Bagthorpe had weakly agreed that she was sure this was the case. It was pointless to argue with Mrs Fosdyke when she got into her stride on the subject of invisible rays. She believed they were everywhere, pollutinating the atmosphere, leaking from people's fridges, televisions, phones and radios.

' 'Ow do you think all them telly pictures go all over everywhere, all the way from London to your 'ouse? Air waves. You're breathing 'em in the 'ole time, the 'ole air's pollutinated.'

Mrs Fosdyke was sometimes unwittingly quite Green in her

outlook. Any Friend of the Earth would have applauded her use of a hot-water bottle and profound mistrust of anything electrical.

When she had first had a fridge she would switch it off at night, to cut down on the leakage of invisible rays, and wonder why her ice-cream was always soft. When Mrs Pye had enlightened her, and given dark warnings about the practice, she had had to choose between invisible rays and salmonella. Even then, it was a close-run thing.

'You 'ave to use natural methods,' she now continued. 'Mrs Bagthorpe and Mrs Bagthorpe Senior believe in Breathing, but I don't know. I've tried it and can't seem to get the 'ang of it. I dare say it works for them that know 'ow to do it. No, I can't say I believe in Breathing.'

The photographer's sour look seemed to indicate that he, for one, wished that she meant this quite literally.

'There's some swear by counting sheep, but I don't. What's the point in counting them silly things? Any case, since that Daisy Parker got that goat I can't bring myself to think about sheep. I'd be all night thinking of them terrible puddles that goat makes on my best Wilton, and all that desiccation 'e done when 'e was drunk. Oh yes. Drunk. Can you believe it? Scottish whisky that Daisy give 'im. Any'ow, I don't count sheep, nor anything else, either. If you counted rabbits, you'd only end up thinking about mixytosis and 'orrible diseases. Same with cows, of course. You wouldn't believe what you can catch eating them. Brussels something. Nor chickens, either. Only supposed to count 'em after they're 'atched, let alone all that salmonella.'

By now both Mrs Fosdyke's listeners (or rather, all three of them, for Patsy Page had re-entered, and was listening in bewilderment) were beginning to feel their own eyes glaze over.

'There's some that swear by listening to waterfalls, and the sea,' continued Mrs Fosdyke, 'and good luck to 'em, I say. But

24

if you really want to know what sends me off, it's them Party Political Broadcasts. You can drop off in your chair in front of one of them. So I just listens to this voice going on and on about 'ow good the National 'Ealth is, and green sprouts and toilets on motorways, and I'm off in no time.'

'Look,' said the photographer wearily, 'haven't we got enough?'

Patsy Page hesitated. She had not only just filed an Exclusive, but was certain that in Mrs Fosdyke she had discovered a Personality. So far she was ahead of the field, but at any moment the rest of the ratpack could descend and camp themselves on the doorstep. If so, Mrs Fosdyke would almost certainly talk to them. On present showing, she was unstoppable. She needed a minder.

'Er – Mrs Bagthorpe? Could I just have a word?'

'Certainly,' replied Mrs Bagthorpe, who in her present state would probably have given the same reply had someone asked if she would mind just poking her finger into a live socket.

The pair withdrew to the kitchen.

'Do you live here?' asked Patsy Page, who had been unable so far to work out just who Mrs Bagthorpe was, and why she was here.

'I have run off from home,' replied Mrs Bagthorpe guilelessly.

The reporter was enchanted by this revelation.

'Battered wife?' she inquired hopefully, scenting another story.

'In a sense. It was the sucked-up sock, you see.'

Ms Page most certainly did not see. She was quite fogged. There was definitely a story here, but it must wait. In the mean time, she thought it prudent to take Mrs Bagthorpe's address, just in case she had disappeared by morning.

'Unicorn House, Passingham.' She noted it down. 'Mmm. Bagthorpe. Sounds familiar.'

25

'It is often in the papers,' Mrs Bagthorpe told her. 'And my husband is Henry Bagthorpe, the screenwriter.'

'That's it!' exclaimed the reporter. 'Saw his last series – the one about that writer tormented by his family.'

'I have watched it seventeen times,' said Mrs Bagthorpe.

The reporter began to see why she had run off from home.

'So you'll be staying here tonight?' she asked.

Mrs Bagthorpe had not given the matter any thought. Under normal circumstances she would have profound misgivings about spending the night under Mrs Fosdyke's roof. Now, it seemed as good an idea as any.

'I expect so,' she replied.

'Good, good. I mean – could you just keep any eye on things?'

'What kind of things?'

'The main thing is to stop her doing any more interviews. When I go back in there I'm going to make her a payment. She'll be under exclusive contract to us. If she talks, there'll be grief.'

'Oh, I expect I can manage that,' Mrs Bagthorpe told her optimistically.

'Quite a character, isn't she? Known her long?'

'Ages,' said Mrs Bagthorpe. 'She is virtually one of the family.'

'Tomorrow we'll see about getting a phone put in. How d'you think she'd react to the idea of a telex?'

'Very badly,' replied Mrs Bagthorpe. 'And you'll have to explain to her that only outgoing calls are charged on the telephone.'

'Oh, we'll pick up the tab for that,' said Ms Page. 'She's a cool old cookie, that's for sure. Jeez – IRA terrorist in her front room – there's plenty'd be under sedation.'

Mrs Bagthorpe forbore to mention that the supposed terrorist was in fact Mrs Fosdyke's own son, who was now upstairs. She had her own sights set on him.

'Right – I'll dole her out some cash on account and get off. There'll have to be an editorial conference, and quick. Who'd have my job? Still a mite confused, truth to tell.'

Mrs Bagthorpe said nothing. When it came to confusion, she probably held the world record in dealing with it. She'd been there, done that. She had the T-shirt.

Three

Jack got up early next day, despite having had a late night. In the end, the other three had called him back in as arbitrator in the Breath Holding Contest. They were all accusing one another of cheating.

'You watch William!' Rosie told Jack. 'He keeps taking little sucks in – I've seen him!'

'Garbage,' said William.

'I must have the most powerful lungs of anyone here,' Tess said. 'You need breath control for the oboe.'

'I don't actually think Breath Holding will count as a String to anyone's Bow,' offered Jack, in the hope of cooling things.

'Don't be an idiot,' William told him. 'It will if I get into *The Guinness Book of Records*.'

'What d'you mean *you*?' screamed Rosie. 'It'll be me – I'm best at it, I am!'

Things had been further complicated by the arrival of Grandma and Daisy. They had had their Chinese takeaway, and were now thirsty. Both perked up on learning what was afoot.

'I'll do it! I'll do it!' squeaked Daisy. 'I can stop breaving for ever and ever if I want to!'

'Amen to that,' said William grimly. He had not forgiven her for piercing his drum with a knife and fork.

'I have been doing a lot of Breathing lately,' Grandma said. 'I dare say this has strengthened my lungs.'

'I honestly think you're too old, Grandma,' Jack said.

She gave him a frosty look.

'Where is your father?' she demanded. 'And why is he not in prison?'

'Uncle Parker got him out,' Jack said. 'And the tramp.'

'Then where is Mr O'Toole?'

'Gone to Uncle Park's.'

'Oooh, he's at our house!' Daisy squealed. 'I want to go home! I want to go home!'

The Bagthorpes' car was still in the police pound. Even had it been in the drive, Mrs Bagthorpe was not there to act as chauffeur, and Mr Bagthorpe would have refused point blank to do so. (He was in any case by now probably over the limit.)

'We will go first thing in the morning, Daisy darling,' Grandma told her. 'We will go over and fetch him back here. He is, after all, one of Albert's oldest friends.'

She had told this fib so many times now that she had almost come to believe it.

'Look, are we holding our breaths or not?' demanded Rosie.

'I is, I is!' Daisy's grasshopper mind was successfully distracted. 'One two free – go!'

She drew in an almighty breath. She held it. And held it. The rest watched with varying degrees of admiration and disgust. Her cheeks puffed out like the north wind. Her face grew redder and redder, her eyes popped. Rosie, for one, was slightly alarmed. She doted on Daisy, but did not fancy the prospect of being beaten by her at Breath Holding.

'She'll bust!' said William hopefully.

At last the air was let out in a long, noisy raspberry.

'Crikey, Daisy, that was brilliant!' said Jack, who alone did not feel threatened by this demonstration. 'And you're only four! That's really interesting. '

'I can't imagine why,' said Tess coldly.

'It could mean that people get born with really elastic lungs, and then they sort of harden up as you get older.'

His siblings were unimpressed by this unscientific theory.

'You do talk rot, Jack,' his brother told him.

'Well, if it's true, my lungs'd be better than yours,' Jack said. He usually avoided Bagthorpian rows, but was now in danger of being drawn into this one. 'But it so happens that I don't *want* to hold my breath.'

'Did I win did I win?' Daisy was jumping up and down.

'I think you probably will, Daisy,' Jack told her. He was fed up with the others, and felt like needling them. They hadn't cared tuppence that their father was in gaol, and were now sitting round holding their breaths when their mother was still missing. He picked up the stop-watch.

'Perhaps I will sit this one out,' said Grandma (who could not work out any way of cheating at this activity). 'I don't wish to spoil darling Daisy's chances.'

In the end, Daisy had won. After the first round everyone said it was a fluke, and it should be best of three – then five, then seven. They hoped that, with being so young, she would tire easily and her performance deteriorate. They should have known better. Daisy did not tire easily. It was the people around her who tended to do that.

'Splendid, Daisy, splendid!' crooned Grandma, when Daisy finally emerged victor, best of fifty-one. She wished she had put money on it.

'I expect she was cheating,' said Tess jealously. 'Jack wasn't watching her properly.'

'I couldn't watch her *and* William,' he objected. '*And* the stop-watch.'

'It was only a piddling game, anyway,' William said.

The three defeated contenders stamped moodily up to bed.

'I winned I winned!' crowed Daisy after them.

Jack opted to wait for the hot milky drink Grandma proposed

to make. He thought (in unconscious unison with Mrs Fosdyke) that it might help him sleep.

'D'you think Mother's all right?' he asked.

At this point his father appeared, thirsty and bad-tempered.

'Der's dat nasty Uncle Bag,' remarked Daisy, mercifully unheard by him.

'Of course she's all right!' he snapped. 'Why wouldn't she be?'

'People usually worry when people go missing,' Jack said. He had no real knowledge of how an ordinary family would react to such a disappearance, but felt sure this must be so.

'She hasn't gone missing,' Mr Bagthorpe said. 'She's just not here, that's all. And just wait till she is. Would you believe I nearly got done for murdering her?'

Grandma, who had skilfully planted the seeds of this suspicion in the police officers' fertile minds, was disappointed that the ploy had not succeeded.

'I expect you are still under suspicion,' she said. 'I expect that they have let you out so that they can watch you, and wait for you to make a false move.'

'Bilge, Mother,' he replied. 'That mutton-headed lot couldn't sniff out a corpse if it was lying stiff in their own cells.'

'Did they ask who her dentist is?' Jack asked.

His father stared.

'Did they *what*? They asked me damn all everything else. How tall, colour of eyes, colour of hair – how the hell did they expect *me* to know, for God's sake!'

'Most people know the colouring of their spouses, Henry,' Grandma told him piously. 'I could certainly describe the colour of dear Albert's eyes.'

'Oh *stop* it!' Jack burst out uncharacteristically. 'I'm worried, if you're not!'

He had left them to wrangle over their hot milky drinks. It had taken him ages to get to sleep. He kept seeing pictures of

31

his mother being held hostage by an IRA bomber, or wandering alone, shell-shocked and suffering from amnesia. Even when he did drop off he was haunted by nightmares.

Now, as he made his way downstairs, he could actually sense Mrs Bagthorpe's absence. At this time she would usually be doing her Yoga and Breathing to prepare her for the rigours of the day ahead. Or she might already be in the kitchen, making tea. The paper was lying on the hall floor and he mechanically stooped and picked it up as he passed.

Had the Bagthorpes subscribed to the *Sludge*, the mystery of his mother's disappearance would have been solved there and then. At that very moment millions were reading the headline – FEARLESS FOZZY FOILS FIEND – and turning to two more pages of reporting and photographs, some of them showing Mrs Bagthorpe in Mrs Fosdyke's living-room.

Unfortunately, the Bagthorpes took the *Guardian*. The *Sludge* had an exclusive on the Fosdyke story, but in any case the *Guardian* would have allocated little space to it, given that its social implications were nil. Even the Knaresborough Knifer sighting had only a column inch on page two (though a *Guardian* man had been on the Aysham Police Station doorstep along with the rest of the media).

'We've got to find Mother,' Jack told Zero. 'We'll start in the garden, then work outwards.'

He did not really believe that Mrs Bagthorpe was now a body, but could not think of anything else he could usefully do. If she had fled to India, for instance, or even Scotland, then nobody would find her. He had noticed that when the police searched for missing persons, they usually found them (after several days) barely two hundred yards from their own homes.

'And she could be unconscious,' he thought. 'She could have tripped and banged her head and gone unconscious.'

So he and Zero set out on their search.

'It needn't be a fingertip search,' Jack told him. 'In any case, you need a whole row of people for that. You just sniff in among the bushes and, if you find anything, bark.'

Zero was already sniffing in among the bushes anyway. Jack looked first in the garage, then the potting-shed and greenhouse. He then made his way to the pool, now known in the family as the Dead Sea.

Both Mr Bagthorpe and his sister swore by goldfish-watching as a way of calming oneself, but would find little joy here. There was little joy for anybody. Not a goldfish was left alive in its curdled waters.

'It's going sour,' Jack thought. 'The milk's gone off and turned to cottage cheese.'

If so, it was certainly not of a wholesome variety. The water-lilies were beginning to curl up at the edges, and looked as if they were going the same way as the goldfish. Daisy had, after all, diligently emptied at least forty pints of milk into the water, with the intention of building up the fish.

Jack tended not to blame Daisy for this. After all, milk was supposed to be good for humans. He could see the way her mind had worked.

He thought it unlikely that his mother had ended up in there, but in the interests of thoroughness prodded around in it with a stick, thereby further curdling the contents.

He combed the garden, coming across parts of it he had almost forgotten. At the Highgate Cemetery end, some of Daisy's makeshift memorials from her Funerals Phase still stood, askew and forlorn. Beneath them lay decaying mutton and pork chops. There was no sign of a memorial recently erected for Mrs Bagthorpe. Zero did no more sniffing there than anywhere else. He did not go in for burying and digging up bones.

'She's not here, old chap,' Jack told him. 'Let's try the meadow.'

He climbed over the stile and Zero crept under the fence, tail well down, and licking his lips. He had always been made nervous by rabbits, and not so long ago had been flushed out of the bushes here by two trained police alsatians.

'Good *boy*!' Jack told him. 'You're really brave. Those police dogs could've killed you. You ought really to have had counselling.'

Zero's tail stirred feebly in response to this patting, and his eyes flicked nervously about.

'You're returning to the scene of the disaster,' Jack went on. 'Like people going straight back up on planes after they've crashed. You're conquering your fear, looking it straight between the eyes. Just try to take deep breaths and keep calm.'

He struck off across the meadow towards the nearest clump of bushes. He could see at a glance that his mother was not there, but beat the grass with his stick, hoping for a clue. Something caught his eye. He bent and picked it up.

'A cash card!'

It was not his mother's.

'Mrs E. Wright,' he read. 'What's that doing here?'

Mrs E. Wright, whoever she was, could hardly have mistaken a hawthorn for a cashpoint. Jack tried hard to make a connection between the find and his missing mother.

'What if she came here to meet someone with a Problem?'

He knew that this was not really on. Stella Bright communicated with her clients only by letter, and advice on her Problem Page. Sometimes she was made quite desperate by this.

'How I long to comfort them!' she would say, after a particularly harrowing mail bag. 'How I long to stretch out a hand!'

It could just be a friend she came to meet. This, too, was a non-starter. None of the Bagthorpes had any friends. For one thing they didn't have time for them – Friendship was unlikely to count as a String to anyone's Bow.

Another far-fetched scenario was that this Mrs Wright had lured Mrs Bagthorpe to the meadow and done away with her.

'It could still be a clue,' he thought, and pocketed the card. He looked at his watch.

'Breakfast time. Where's Fozzy?' he looked hopefully in the direction of the village for the sight of that familiar, scuttling figure. Then he remembered Mrs Fosdyke's unaccountable appearance on the television screen the previous evening.

'That bomb! I bet she's got shock and not coming in!'

This was a dispiriting thought. Although the Bagthorpes were now reduced to doing their own housework, at least there had been Mrs Fosdyke's cooking to look forward to. She had regarded it as Occasional Thurpy, as prescribed by her doctor for the nervous breakdown she claimed to be suffering.

Jack wondered whether he should go over to Coldharbour Road and offer his sympathy. His stomach rumbled.

'Breakfast,' he decided.

He turned and went back to Unicorn House with the intention of having a good fry-up. This was not allowed, except on rare occasions. His mother was very keen on a low-fat diet, and allowed only boiled or scrambled eggs, and muesli. Mrs Fosdyke always had bacon in, however, and if his luck was in he might find sausages, too.

His disappointment when he could find neither of these things was keen. He remembered the fry-up his heartless siblings had been having when he had set off for the police station in Aysham.

'Greedy things! They've pigged the lot! And no mushrooms, either, or tomatoes.' He felt quite murderous.

Rosie came in, still in her nightshirt.

'Where's Fozzy?' she asked.

'I don't expect she's coming in. Not after that bomb.'

Rosie stared. Last night everyone had been too busy holding their breath and having fry-ups to keep abreast of the news.

'She was on telly. I saw her. Something about a terrorist in her front room, and a bomb.'

'But who'd want to blow her up?' (The answer to that, of course, was Rosie's own father. He, however, had a cast-iron alibi in that he was holed up in a police cell at the time.)

'You've scoffed all the bacon, pigs!'

'But if she's not coming in, who'll do the cooking?'

'Mother, I expect,' Jack said. 'Except that she's not here, either.'

'What's she want to go off like that for, leaving us in the lurch?' said Rosie crossly.

'I think it was Father sucking up that sock.'

'But he's done it before – you know he has – he does it on purpose to get out of hoovering. And now we'll be slaving all day doing cleaning *and* cooking! What about the Strings to my Bow!'

'You certainly didn't get a new one last night,' Jack told her, with intent to wound.

'Just shut up about that! I let Daisy win on purpose.'

'You did not!'

'I did, then!'

'Not!'

At this juncture Mr Bagthorpe entered. He made straight for the fridge and the orange juice.

'Father, Fozzy's not coming in, and . . . '

'We don't *know* that,' Jack interrupted. 'She might, later.'

'Demented hedgehog!' muttered Mr Bagthorpe, meaning Mrs Fosdyke.

'Jack says she was on telly last night.'

'She *what*?'

'Something about a terrorist, and a bomb at her house.'

'I don't believe it,' said Mr Bagthorpe flatly. 'The woman hasn't a drop of Irish blood in her veins. She hasn't got a drop of *human* blood in her veins, she – '

36

'Mother was on, as well,' Jack interrupted.

'*What?*'

'As a Missing Person. There was a photo of her.'

'How many more times do I have to tell you that she isn't missing. Just self-serving attention-seeking.' He was jealous, Jack could see that. He was jealous and mad, and about to get madder.

'*And* you,' Jack went on relentlessly.

'*What?*' *His father whizzed round and a spray of orange juice shot out. 'What?'*

'They didn't say you'd murdered anyone, or anything. Just assaulted a police officer.'

'His hat fell off,' Mr Bagthorpe said. 'I was just moving past him, and his hat fell off. It was wrongful arrest. I'll sue.'

'No one's listening to me,' said Rosie, with perfect truth. 'If Fozzy doesn't come in, who'll do the cooking?'

'You will,' he told her. 'You lot will. What's the matter with you? Anyone can cook.'

'*You* can't,' she told him. 'You can't even boil an egg. And don't give us all that bilge about being a sensitive creative writer, because we don't believe it.'

Mr Bagthorpe, who had indeed opened his mouth to plead exemption on the grounds of the demands of his calling, closed it again.

'If she doesn't come in she's in breach of contract,' he said, after a pause. 'Get on the phone and tell her to get in here, fast.'

'She's not on the phone,' Rosie reminded him.

'She doesn't believe in them,' Jack added.

'Then one of you get over there and fetch her.'

'Bags not me!' said Rosie and Jack simultaneously. Mrs Fosdyke would in all likelihood slam the door in their faces. Last time they had visited her at home they had come bearing maggots. This was not their fault (Daisy had placed them in the 'nests' left in a half-eaten box of chocolates), but it was unlikely

37

that Mrs Fosdyke's memory of this horrible shock had faded.

Billy Goat Gruff entered the kitchen. He came tap-tapping in on his fastidious hoofs. He stopped, stood there, and quite deliberately made a puddle. The trio stared in disbelief. No one had bothered to keep track of his movements, as they would have normally.

'You mean to tell me that all-fired beast has been all night in my house?'

This conclusion seemed inescapable.

'Daisy's still asleep in my room,' Rosie said. 'She must be exhausted with all that Breath Holding.'

The fact that Daisy was still in bed at nine o'clock in the morning seemed to point to the fact that she had stopped breathing altogether. Such a thing was virtually unknown. She was usually up and doing at the crack of dawn.

'Well, get her up,' ordered Mr Bagthorpe. 'We'll bang her and the goat straight back to Russell's.'

'We haven't got a car,' Jack pointed out.

'Let him fetch her – and that accursed goat.'

'He hasn't, either,' Jack reminded him. 'He left it outside the police station when he came to rescue you.'

It was now, in fact, in the police pound alongside the Bagthorpes' own.

'And don't say she can walk, 'cos she can't,' said Rosie. 'She's only little.'

'She's little like a scorpion's little,' her father said. 'Lend her a bike, get a taxi, anything, but get her off my premises.'

'She won't want to stop anyway, when she finds out there are no proper meals,' Rosie said. 'I might go with her.'

'You stop where you are and get some recipe books out,' he told her.

'I don't mind having a go at cooking,' Jack said.

'You keep out of it,' said his father brutally.

Tess and William came down, also in search of breakfast.

They were disgusted to hear of Mrs Fosdyke's defection. They were also inclined to think that Jack had imagined the whole business about the bomb, or made it up.

'She'll just be having one of her nervies,' William said. 'You go over there, Jack, and butter her up. She likes you best. Hey – what's that goat doing?'

The goat was chewing at a string of garlic bulbs that hung by the stove. There was a pungent reek that reminded them of the ghost-hunting days in Wales. This was not something that anyone wished to be reminded of.

'Stinking brute,' observed Tess. 'Is that one of his puddles? Where's Daisy?'

People usually asked this, not out of any concern for her safety and well-being, but because they felt safer when they knew her whereabouts. They knew whether or not to watch their backs.

'In bed,' Jack told him. 'She's probably tired. She's a bit young to do all that Breath Holding.'

At that moment the telephone rang.

'Could be Mother!' Jack ran into the hall to answer it. 'Hello, Jack Bagthorpe here.'

'Oooh!' he heard a voice say. 'I think it's working!'

'Hello?'

It was definitely not his mother, but it might be someone with news of her.

' 'E's a bit muffled, but it's Jack, I'm sure it is! Should I pull this silver stick out a bit more, d'you think?'

He now thought he knew who the caller was.

'Mrs Fosdyke? Mrs Fosdyke?'

'Oooh, it *is* 'im! I can't 'ardly believe it! No wires or nothing and I'm not even connected!'

'Mrs Fosdyke?'

'Yes, all right, I'm going to.' A clearing of the throat. ' 'Ello, 'ello. Mrs Fosdyke speaking.'

'Yes, I know. Are you all right? Where are you?' Surely not at home?

'I'm at 'ome, in the kitchen, on account of all them round the front.'

'At *home*? But – you haven't got a phone!'

'I'm talking into one of them walking telephones. Can you 'ear me?'

'Yes! Yes!'

'In't it wonderful, the things they come up with! I could talk in it upstairs, if I wanted to, or in the garden.'

'Yes, I know – brilliant. But, Mrs Fosdyke, what's happening?'

'I've rung with a message,' she said. 'That Patsy rung the number for me. I ain't coming in today.'

'Oh. Aren't you well?'

'I'm under contract, see. Exclusive.' The note of pride was clearly discernible, even over the crackling line. 'I can't come out the 'ouse.'

Jack was baffled. Mrs Fosdyke's lines of thought had never been easy to follow. Now, they were impenetrable.

'Why can't you?

'We've got all the curtains drawn to stop 'em looking in. They got them telephonic lenses, she says, and'll stop at nothing. It's ever so exciting.'

Mrs Fosdyke sounded anything but ill. She sounded chipper as never before.

'I'm afraid I don't quite understand,' Jack said. 'Will you be in tomorrow?'

'Oh, I shouldn't think so. Not if things go on like this. As a matter of fact,' she paused, overcome with the momentousness of the news, 'as a matter of fact, they might be going to put me in a secret address!'

'A what?'

'You know – a safe 'ouse. Like that Salmon Rushy.' (She

40

pronounced the first name as in the fish.)

'You mean someone's out to *kill* you?'

'There's only me saw that bomber, see.' By now Mrs Fosdyke had quite forgotten that the supposed terrorist was her own son. 'I'm a witness, see. And then there's all them others trying to get to me.'

'What others?'

'I keep telling you – they're all outside the 'ouse. I took a peek through my bedroom curtains – you never seen the like – all over everywhere. Telly and all. And they keep 'ammering on the door.'

Number eleven Coldharbour Road, it seemed, was under siege.

'You won't go anywhere without telling us, will you?' Jack pleaded.

'I shall 'ave to go now,' announced the caller. 'There's all sorts to do, and Patsy wants the phone.'

'Patsy? Who's Patsy?' Jack could not recall her ever mentioning anyone of this name.

'Bye-bye, then,' said Mrs Fosdyke. 'And keep everything under your 'at.'

Click. The line went dead. The call was over. Not once had Jack thought of asking whether Mrs Fosdyke had seen his mother, and not once had that lady thought of mentioning that she was asleep upstairs at number eleven Coldharbour Road. Mrs Bagthorpe was still officially Missing.

Four

Uncle Parker had got up and gone for his usual jog through the dewy meadows, despite the trauma of the previous night.

He had mistakenly thought that he had seen the last of the police for the time being, when he had driven off in the taxi. Instead, they had been on his doorstep within the hour, accusing him of murder (presumably a copycat crime, given that they also believed that Mr Bagthorpe had murdered his wife).

Unfortunately for their theory, the corpse involved had begun to show signs of life within moments of their radioing base for the Murder Squad. The eyelids definitely fluttered. They hoped, rather unsportingly, that this was merely a last tremor. They could not afford to be made to look silly again today – particularly by Uncle Parker.

Uncle Parker was by now cordially hated by the entire Aysham police force, and number one on their hit list. If these two officers could nail him for murder, they would – and become heroes in the process.

'Leave her alone,' one told him. 'You're interfering with evidence. Don't touch that sword.'

Even as he spoke he noted that the weapon was disappointingly free of blood, as was the corpse itself.

'Probably changed his mind, and strangled her,' he thought.

Nor was Aunt Celia blue in the face.

'Or poisoned her, of course. More than one way to kill a cat.'

'I think it's some kind of ritual murder,' his colleague whispered. 'Look at his get-up.'

It was, of course, hideously embarrassing for Uncle Parker to be caught dressed up in one of Mrs Bagthorpe's cast-off frocks. Barefoot and bangled as he was, he could easily have been a member of some occult sect that went in for ritual sacrifice. The music that was still drifting through the house was suspiciously New Age. What ordinary kind of man put on that kind of music before murdering his own wife?

'Russell . . .' murmured the corpse. 'Oh Russell, I thought . . .'

'The doctor'll be here shortly, madam,' one officer said. He did not add 'too late, I hope', but thought it.

'Oh dearest . . .' Uncle Parker leaned over her to catch her whisper.

'I had . . . a visitation . . .' Aunt Celia was trying to recollect what had happened. 'I saw . . . I saw an angel . . .'

To be fair, by now she probably thought she had. Her gaze travelled from her spouse's anxious face to the rest of him. She closed her eyes again, understandably thinking that she must be hallucinating.

The talk of angels and subsequent closing of eyes encouraged the police to believe that the victim was now dead.

'It's this!' exclaimed Uncle Parker, oblivious of anyone or anything but his wife.

With one sweep he pulled the offending frock up over his ears and tossed it aside. His beads and bangles jangled. The police shuffled uneasily. The murderer, possibly a maniac, was now wearing nothing but underpants and assorted geegaws. They decided to keep quiet and await developments. It seemed foolhardy to distract him. There was still a workmanlike-looking sword to hand.

'Celia, Celia, dear heart . . .'

Again the eyelids fluttered.

'What if she doesn't die?' whispered one officer to the other. 'We've called the squad out.'

'Just lingering,' whispered the other. 'Already had one near-death experience. Hear that about angels?'

As they consulted, the murderer swept his victim up in his arms and began to stride from the room.

'Stop!'

'He's tampering with evidence!'

They hurried after him. Uncle Parker kicked open the door of his wife's bower, with the intention of laying her in the white hammock, which might soothe her.

'Hell's bells!' He had forgotten about the goat's field day.

He turned, but not before the police had seen past him. To them, who knew nothing of Billy Goat Gruff, the scene looked definitely like the work of a maniac. The room had been comprehensively destroyed.

'There's two of us to one of him,' whispered One, hoping that things would not come to that.

Uncle Parker went past them and up the stairs. They were not inclined to follow him. They thought they might be safer on the ground floor.

'Best stop and watch the scene of the crime,' said Two. 'If we turn our backs, he could start tampering with evidence.'

They returned to the sitting-room that now, with both corpse and murderer gone, looked disappointingly unlike the scene of a crime. The only unusual items were a crumpled frock and a bloodless sword.

'Can't make head or tail of it,' said One.

'We got here just in time,' said Two. 'Even if she's not dead, she would've been, if we hadn't turned up when we did.'

Even as he spoke, he knew that these words would sound thin in court.

'That stuff he was wearing. What d'you make of that?'

Both shook their heads. They were fogged.

'Kinky, anyhow.' Two voiced his thoughts. 'That's for sure. The jury won't like it.'

'What're we going to get him for if she *doesn't* die?'

'And what're we going to say when Forensic turns up?'

The pair glumly contemplated the bloodless sword and weighed up the possibility of bringing in a conviction for a victimless crime.

Upstairs, Aunt Celia was now as close to ordinary consciousness as she ever was. She even noticed that Uncle Parker was almost naked (though fortunately had no memory of the frock). She begged him to put on some clothes, before he caught a chill.

'You are the father of my unborn twins,' she told him. Uncle Parker little knew how lucky he was to hear this. Given the recent visitation by an angel, he could have been left out of the picture altogether. He padded off to find his dressing-gown.

'This has been a day of days,' she told him dreamily on his return.

'You can say that again,' he agreed with feeling. He remembered the officers downstairs, and that this day of days was not yet over. He decided to see them off before they could alarm his wife.

'You stay here, dear heart,' he told her, 'and I'll go down and fetch some lovely weak, lemony tea.'

She must, after all, be in shock. Even she did not have visitations from angels every day of the week.

'Oh Russell, how truly blessed we are,' she murmured as he left the room.

This was not his own summary of the situation. His mind was working fast. As he passed the devastated bower, he dodged nimbly in and picked up a couple of joss-sticks. Attack was going to be not only the best, but the only, possible form of defence. He strode into the sitting-room.

45

'You still here?' he demanded.

Both officers jumped. One hurriedly positioned himself between Uncle Parker and the sword. Ignoring them, he went over to a vase of flowers, stuck one of the joss-sticks in, and lit it. He crossed over to another floral arrangement and did the same.

'Off, now, are you?' he inquired. 'Satisfied?'

The music stopped. The sudden silence was unnerving.

'You burst into my house, without a warrant, and frighten my wife almost to death. I may or may not press charges.'

'What about the sword?' asked One. 'What about you dressed up in that?' He indicated the discarded frock.

'I do not have to explain to you what I do in the privacy of my own home,' replied Uncle Parker. 'If I wished, I could dance the hornpipe naked on the kitchen table. However, it so happens that my wife and myself were about to do a spot of meditation. Any law against that, is there?'

The officers looked uneasily at the joss-sticks with their thinly wreathing smoke. The connection they had made was not with meditation, but drugs.

'All right, then,' said Two. 'What about all that business in the bushes? I take it it was you?'

'Certainly,' replied Uncle Parker. 'I was poking around in my own bushes in my own drive in the hopes of retrieving that.'

He nodded towards the cast-off frock.

'And what was it doing there, sir?'

'My nephew put it there. Young Jack Bagthorpe.'

The officers winced. As far as they were concerned, the word 'trouble' began with a B.

'Belongs to a guest of ours,' continued Uncle Parker, 'or rather he was, till that damn-fool taxi-driver made off with him.'

'In that case,' said One, 'what were you doing wearing it?'

'I always slip into something loose when I meditate,' Uncle Parker informed him. 'Saved me going up for this.' He indicated his swish silk dressing-gown. 'Any more silly questions?'

There was only one line of inquiry left.

'The sword. What about the sword?'

'I'll tell you what about the sword. And it is at this point that I am tempted to forget that I am a law-abiding citizen, and assault a police officer. Throughout the day reports have been broadcast about the Knaresborough Knifer being in the vicinity. Those reports originated from Aysham police. As a result, your own station is surrounded by the mass media, and sensitive, highly strung ladies such as my wife have been frightened into fits. It was in an attempt to calm her that we were about to embark on a stint of meditation. Even then, she insisted that I have a weapon to hand should the Knifer break in.' He nodded towards the sword. 'A perfectly natural response, I should have thought. In the event, it was not the Knifer, but yourselves, who rendered her insensible with shock.'

Put like that, it all sounded quite feasible.

'It is to be hoped no real damage has been done,' continued Uncle Parker. 'My wife is in a delicate condition. She is expecting twins.'

This settled it. Neither officer wished to assist at a premature birth, though they had, naturally, received training for such an emergency. They felt they had had enough for one day. They left. As soon as they got outside they radioed through and cancelled the Murder Squad. Uncle Parker locked and bolted the door behind them, made the lovely weak, lemony tea, and called it a day.

Now, as he jogged through the dewy meadows, he planned his agenda for the day ahead. The first priority was to retrieve his car. Then, of course, there was Mr O'Toole to track down. He cursed the taxi-driver who had abducted him.

'Had him in the bag,' he thought. 'Could be anywhere now.'

The only comfort was that Aunt Celia, since seeing the angel, had not mentioned the tramp. Uncle Parker was not as disturbed by the angel as some husbands might have been. Indeed, he thought it a vast improvement on the tramp, in that angels did not, so far as he was aware, stink, *or* consume vast quantities of malt whisky.

It was unlikely that his wife would wake before noon. She needed between eight and twelve hours of sleep. Uncle Parker would explain to people that this was to restore her delicate nervous system, upon which the crudity of the world had jarred throughout the day. Mr Bagthorpe said that it was lucky, in that case, that his sister did not go to work, like any ordinary mortal.

'Let her try getting up at seven and stacking shelves in Tesco's,' he would say. 'That'd fix her nervous system.'

Uncle Parker said that sleeping *was* his wife's work. It was a necessary part of her poetry and pottery. Without her dreams she could not follow her calling. She kept a notebook by her bed, and would faithfully record them, even in the middle of the night. They might otherwise fade and dissolve, she said, like foam upon the deep.

Mr Bagthorpe was equally dismissive about the dreaming.

'Celia's life is one long dream,' he asserted. 'She fell asleep at birth, and hasn't woken since. She's a zombie, one of the walking dead. I don't know what it'll take to wake her up. I've tried, God knows.'

He further maintained that his sister's sleepwalking through life was probably the source of Daisy's delinquency. With her mother more or less permanently out to lunch, Daisy was effectively living in a one-parent family. Given that Uncle Parker was that parent, and unfit to care for a goldfish, let alone a child, there was little wonder his daughter already had a criminal record as long as your arm. There was as yet no secure prison for under-fives, but doubtless the Home Secretary had the matter in hand.

'If she goes unchecked and is still on the loose at seven, it'll be Armageddon,' he said. 'The whole fabric of society will be torn apart.'

Now, given that Aunt Celia had had both her nursery and bower destroyed, and been visited by an angel, all in one day, Uncle Parker thought a good long sleep was definitely on the cards. His wife had been too excited to go to sleep much before midnight. It was the angel that had really got to her – she had even started describing it. Apparently it had green eyes.

He left a note by her bed, along with the single perfect rose he presented to her each day. (He continued this practice even during the winter months, thereby running up a hefty florist's bill.) He then ordered a taxi, and told the driver to go first to Unicorn House. There he found the family in the kitchen, discussing Mrs Fosdyke's phone call.

'A *mobile* phone?' Rosie shrieked when Jack relayed the news. 'Fozzy? You're joking!'

'She said the house was besieged by reporters. And she might be going to a safe house. You know – like Salman Rushdie.'

Mr Bagthorpe was annoyed that someone should have thought of taking out a fatwa against Mrs Fosdyke before he did.

'She said she was under contract. Exclusive.'

'She's under contract to come in here and get cooking,' his father said.

At this point Uncle Parker entered. They were caught off guard by his arrival, unheralded by the usual spurt of gravel.

'Good morning, all,' he greeted them. 'Ah – Henry. Recovering from your ordeal? I must say I've never seen you as a gaolbird.'

'Your accursed daughter is still under my roof,' Mr Bagthorpe countered. 'Get her out – fast. And that all-fired goat.'

'Any sign of Laura?' inquired Uncle Parker.

49

'Does it look like it?'

'Plenty to run away from, of course,' said Uncle Parker. 'Poor Laura.'

'And now Fozzy's not coming in,' Rosie told him. 'What are we going to eat?'

'Just popping into Aysham to spring my car,' Uncle Parker said. 'Care for a lift, Henry?'

'If I want to go anywhere I'll drive myself,' he replied ungratefully.

'You can't – your car's gone missing,' Jack reminded him.

Mr Bagthorpe was genuinely floored by this. He really had forgotten about his car. He was the exception that proves the rule that all men subconsciously identify with their cars, that their whole identity is threatened if anything happens to them. He felt threatened all right, but not by that.

'Go and get it, Father,' William urged. 'Without a car we shall be sunk. We won't even be able to fetch takeaways.'

'Do you think of anything but your stomachs?' Mr Bagthorpe asked. 'I've told you – get cooking!'

'Mrs Fosdyke says she's besieged,' Jack said. 'By the media.'

'Besieged, eh?' said Uncle Parker. 'Sounds as if Mrs Fosdyke's something of a star. It'll be you next, Henry.'

'Why will it? he demanded. '*I* don't see terrorists under the bed.'

'Ah, but your wife has gone missing,' Uncle Parker reminded him. 'The press like that. Got an alibi?'

'I just hope they do come,' Jack said. 'It's about time someone started looking for Mother.'

'If reporters do come, I'm going to tell them about Anonymous from Grimsby,' William said. 'That'll make a good story.'

'Then I could show them my portraits,' piped up Rosie. 'They could do me as a Child Prodigy.'

'There is certainly a wave of interest in the paranormal,' Tess said. 'I could tell them about my experiments.'

Mr Bagthorpe was predictably disgusted.

'What miserable wretches you are,' he told them. 'The last thing any of you need is the oxygen of publicity.'

'Ah, but you could do with it, Henry,' Uncle Parker told him. 'For a writer, any publicity is good publicity, eh?'

'I wouldn't have thought assaulting police officers was good publicity for anybody,' William said.

'*Or* not even bothering to look for Mother,' Jack added.

Mr Bagthorpe was beginning to feel cornered. His mind worked rapidly. If he got his car back, then returned to Unicorn House to find the nation's press camped on the doorstep, he could execute a smart U-turn and head for Great-Aunt Lucy in Torquay. He only ever did this as a last resort, but things were beginning to feel as if he'd need a last resort. He was now torn between his natural stinginess and a deep reluctance to share a taxi with Uncle Parker. There again, the press could already be on their way. By the time he had called for his own taxi and waited for it to arrive, it could be too late.

'I haven't got time to stand around bandying words,' he said. 'I'm off to fetch the car. Coming, Russell?' He managed to make it sound as if the taxi had been his own idea.

'Cheers, all!' Uncle Parker followed him out.

'Let's have a good fry-up,' suggested William in the silence that followed.

'You had that last night,' Jack told him. 'There's no bacon, and no sausages.'

'There won't be any lunch, either,' said Rosie glumly. 'No Fozzy. It's all right Father saying get the recipe books out. There's more to cooking than recipes.'

'There shouldn't be,' said Tess thoughtfully. 'A recipe book is simply an instruction manual. Anyone should be able to follow it. And cookery would certainly count as an extra String to my Bow.'

This, to two of her siblings at least, sounded ominous. At

present they were more or less neck and neck as regards Strings to Bows.

'I'll have a go,' William said. 'Any fool can do it.'

'*And* me,' said Rosie. 'I've helped Fozzy lots of times.'

This was not strictly true. All it meant was that she, as youngest, could vaguely remember times spent in the kitchen sticking Smarties into icing on buns, and licking spoons. She had also cut out gingerbread men, and attempted the odd *Blue Peter* cake.

At this point Grandma entered.

'Where have your father and Russell gone in that taxi?' she inquired without preliminary.

'To fetch their cars,' Jack told her.

'Fozzy's not coming in, so we're going to cook,' said Rosie.

'Why is that?' asked Grandma, who had herself not seen Mrs Fosdyke's television interview the previous evening. 'I really have heard quite enough about that ridiculous nervous breakdown.'

'Something to do with her being a witness,' Jack said. 'And loads of reporters outside her house.'

'Perhaps one of you could make me some toast,' said Grandma. 'Just nicely browned, thank you. Where is darling Daisy?'

'Still in bed,' Rosie told her. 'She looked really sweet, so I didn't wake her.'

Grandma was slightly alarmed by this intelligence. Such behaviour was quite untypical.

'It is to be hoped she is not sickening for something,' she said.

'Or having a nervous breakdown,' said Tess, and the others tittered.

'Aren't you going to ask about Mother?' Jack was by now thoroughly fed up by the way people were treating her disappearance.

52

'I expect she is just doing what Agatha Christie did,' remarked Grandma calmly. 'I expect she is in a hotel in Harrogate waiting to be found.'

'Harrogate?' Jack stared.

'I think we should leave her there a little longer,' Grandma continued. 'The household runs perfectly smoothly without her.'

'Well *I* don't think it does! And I miss her, even if nobody else does, and I think you're all rotten, just sitting round talking about food when she might be dead!'

With this Jack ran from the room before anyone could spot the shaming moistness of his eyes. A Bagthorpe never cried. Hell might freeze over, the sun shine blood-red at noon, but a Bagthorpe never, ever cried.

Five

Mrs Fosdyke had hardly been exaggerating when she described the state of affairs in Coldharbour Road. For the second time in twenty-four hours it was swarming with the mass media. On this occasion, it was Mrs Fosdyke herself who was News. She had quite eclipsed the supposed terrorist bomber. Her radio and television interviews the previous day had, it seemed, gone straight to the heart of the nation.

On Radio Four's *PM* programme she had scored a direct hit, particularly with her tip about refrigerated knitting. The BBC had been desperate to do a follow-up on the *Today* programme, but had been foiled by the wily Patsy Page. Rival news editors had seen the coverage in the *Sludge* and recognized a scoop when they saw it. They had summoned their top reporters and issued urgent instructions.

'Find the old bat and get her talking,' they were told. 'Get her opinions. On anything.'

So far the *Sludge* had published Mrs Fosdyke's opinions only about telephones and insomnia. This left a wide field yet to be covered.

'Ask her about the rise in crime, the Royal Family, UFOs. Just get her talking. Oh – and get some pictures.'

One or two early birds had managed a few long-range shots of Mrs Fosdyke in curlers and dressing-gown before the curtains were drawn. Once Patsy Page (recognized by the entire press corps) had driven up, gone inside and set about drawing curtains, strong dissatisfaction and resentment set in. It was unethical, the other reporters said, to hijack a news story in this high-handed way. Several of them wanted to bug the house, but by now an inhabitant of Coldharbour Road had rung the police, and one of their number was parked near by, reading his own *Sludge* and eating sandwiches.

Inside number eleven was a state of affairs more newsworthy than any of them could have guessed. Mrs Bagthorpe, now in her second day of being Missing, was steadily climbing towards the headlines. Mrs Fosdyke, besides being a charismatic Personality, was also conspiring to pervert the course of justice, and harbouring a wanted felon.

By now Patsy Page was aware that Mrs Bagthorpe was the missing Stella Bright, and that she had unwittingly scored a second Exclusive. She could already see herself as Reporter of the Year. She wanted to get Mrs Bagthorpe straight down for an interview, but Mrs Fosdyke proved surprisingly resistant to this.

'You let 'er sleep it out,' she said. 'She 'as an 'orrible time at 'ome, and there's no wonder she's run off. Bucketfuls of dead goldfish, fires being lit all over everywhere and that Daisy Parker and 'er goat.'

'Er – why are there bucketfuls of dead goldfish, Mrs Fosdyke?' asked Patsy Page.

'Overdose of milk,' Mrs Fosdyke explained. 'That Daisy Parker, of course. Not fit to be loose. Ought to be locked up.'

Patsy Page scented another story.

Upstairs, Mrs Bagthorpe was slowly returning to consciousness. She opened her eyes and saw dangling above her a livid green lampshade fringed with orange. She closed them again. Slowly she became aware that she was not in her own bed. Usually, in the very moment of waking, she tried to have a Positive Thought. 'This will be a happy, happy day' or 'All things work together for good' were two such thoughts she clung to in the face of all evidence to the contrary. Now, she could not seem to think of a single inspiring *mot*. She could not, indeed, even remember who she was, let alone where. She seemed to have run off the tracks.

Most people would just have lain there and let things wash over them, but old habits died hard. Mrs Bagthorpe bravely opened her eyes again and sat up.

'Psst!'

A hiss drew her eyes to the doorway. There, having evidently slept in his clothes, was Max. She stared. He put a warning finger to his lips. His eyes were wide and scared. Here was a fellow human being in distress.

'I think they're on to me!' His voice was hoarse.

'Max!'

All at once she remembered who she was and what she had to do. She was a composite of Stella Bright, Agony Aunt and magistrate on the Aysham Bench. Here was a poor, terrified creature who had in a desperate moment stolen and used a cash card, and now needed her help. Her face broke into a smile so radiant that Max, startled, peered over his shoulder to see who it was she was greeting.

'The fuzz! I seen 'em!'

'Now, Max, you have nothing to fear,' she began.

'Sshh!' he hissed again. 'Keep yer voice down! Mum's got someone down there with 'er.'

Now Mrs Bagthorpe remembered the previous evening, and Patsy Page. She obligingly reduced her voice to a whisper.

'She knows nothing of you,' she told him naïvely. The *Sludge* reporter was at that very moment noticing photographs of an infant Max in his pram or high chair.

'I've got to get out of 'ere!'

A night spent tossing and turning in a roomful of stuffed toys and embalmed dummies had had an unsettling effect. He had half expected some of the pink rabbits to start talking, and

56

could swear he had seen a couple of them move. He was having trouble with his identity. If his own mother did not know him, who did?

'It would certainly be best,' Mrs Fosdyke agreed. 'For one thing, you need a good tidy-up.'

Max mistook her meaning.

'I could dye me 'air yellow,' he said eagerly. 'And I could grow a beard! And a moustache!'

'Oh no!' said Mrs Bagthorpe hastily, knowing the effect such a transformation would have on her fellow members on the Bench. 'Simply – a tidy-up. And a change of clothes.'

Even at a distance her nose was picking up a smell that seemed vaguely familiar. Then she remembered Mr O'Toole – and then she remembered home.

'You must come home with me,' she told him. 'You will be safe there.'

Max, too, was busy remembering. From what he remembered about his mother's remarks about Unicorn House, it was anything but safe (and this even before Daisy Parker had appeared on the scene). She had often said that it was a madhouse, and was turning her hair grey. He realized, however, that at the present moment almost anywhere would be safer than number eleven Coldharbour Road.

'But 'ow?' he asked. ' 'Ow'll we get there? There's dozens of 'em out there!'

'They can't possibly know you are in here,' she told him. 'They are not interested in you.'

This might have been true, but Patsy Page, downstairs, was. She picked up the photographs of the baby and toddling Max and admired them excessively.

'Your grandson?' she asked.

'Son,' said Mrs Fosdyke unguardedly.

'But – ' Patsy Page did some rapid mental calculations and worked out that, in that case, Mrs Fosdyke must be in *The*

Guinness Book of Records. Also, there had so far been no mention of a Mr Fosdyke.

Mrs Fosdyke was doing some rapid thinking of her own. Max had turned up out of the blue, looking like a tramp and on the run from the police. For two pins she would have shopped him. Now, however, she was herself front page headlines, and about to become a star. She had never even dreamed of such a thing, but now that it was happening, she liked it. She felt rather as she imagined the Queen must feel. But she knew all too well what the newspapers would make of a son who went round robbing cash cards from defenceless landladies.

'I shall 'ave to watch what I say,' she told herself.

'And – where is he now?' asked the baffled reporter.

'Oh – just off Pacamac-ing round the world,' replied Mrs Fosdyke vaguely.

This evoked a startling picture of a toddler. Patsy Page realized that she must somehow have got the wrong end of the stick.

'And – how old is he now?' she inquired.

' 'Oo knows?' replied Mrs Fosdyke, sounding as unmaternal as anyone the reporter had yet encountered. Even the mothers of murderers tended to know the ages of their own sons.

'And – when did you last hear news of him?'

Mrs Fosdyke, whatever her faults, was not a very good fibber. The strain of this inquisition began to tell.

'Oooh, 'e sends postcards from all over,' she said. ' 'E's ever such a good son.'

She hoped the paper would print this. It would be nice for the world to think she had a good son.

'And where was the last card from?' probed Ms Page.

'I can't rightly remember.' Mrs Fosdyke was floundering. 'It didn't say.'

'But where was the picture on the card?'

'There – there wasn't one. 'E told me. On the phone.'

58

'But Mrs Fosdyke, you don't have a phone.'

'Oh – nor I don't! Oh dear! 'E must've rung me in a call-box. Yes – that was it!'

'I think you are trying to hide something, Mrs Fosdyke,' said Ms Page reprovingly. 'Don't you think you'd better tell me?'

Mrs Fosdyke hesitated. She naïvely believed that perhaps she could confide in a reporter from the *Sludge* newspaper.

'D'you promise not to tell?' she asked.

Before Patsy Page could perjure herself, Mrs Bagthorpe appeared.

'Good morning, Mrs Fosdyke,' she said, for all the world as if it were a commonplace for her to spend the night there. 'Oh – and good morning Miss – er – '?'

'Page. Patsy Page. Mrs Laura Bagthorpe, isn't it?'

'Well, yes, I have already – '

'Reported Missing. *Alter persona* Stella Bright.'

'Certainly.'

'I wonder – could I have a few words?'

'Certainly,' replied Mrs Bagthorpe. 'But first we must do a deal.' She saw that Ms Page was holding a photo of the toddler Max about to blow out two candles on a cake.

'You have heard about Max?'

'Sure. He sounds great. I really enjoy your page – Stella Bright's always a must for me – I've come near writing to you myself.'

'Really? About Max . . .'

' 'Ave you seen all them reporters outside?' interrupted Mrs Fosdyke, trying to steer conversation in a safer direction.

'Certainly I have,' replied her employer. 'They are causing an obstruction.'

'They're getting me out of 'ere,' confided Mrs Fosdyke. 'Taking me to a safe 'ouse or bungalow. A bungalow'd be nice.'

'For her own protection,' added Patsy Page.

This played neatly into Mrs Bagthorpe's hands.

'Then the sooner you go the better,' she said.

'Oh, no hurry,' the reporter said. She was rather enjoying the feeling of power it gave her to have rivals milling furiously around outside. 'I thought perhaps a brief interview with yourself . . .?'

'I will give you an interview,' Mrs Bagthorpe returned, 'but on my own terms.'

She was going to prove a harder nut to crack than Mrs Fosdyke. Her strategy was already worked out. It was clear that anyone leaving the house at present would be pounced on by the assembled media. Max could not make good his escape until they had gone.

'Mrs Fosdyke, go and pack your case,' she ordered. 'While you are doing so, I will have a chat with Miss Page. You will then both leave the house. Immediately.'

'Oooh, I 'aven't even made a list!' shrieked Mrs Fosdyke, who had liked the idea of decamping in principle, but was now made aware of the immensity of the step.

She did not really like leaving home, and the last time she had done so, to accompany the Bagthorpes to Wales, had entrenched her conviction that there was no place like home.

On the rare occasions when she did go away for a few days, to visit her cousin Doris in Penge, for instance, she packed as if embarking on a six-month safari. When they saw Mrs Fosdyke coming, porters tended to hide behind pillars. She started packing a full fortnight before the date of departure, and always made a list. This was a comprehensive one, because she didn't wish to be caught away from home without some vital commodity. She catered for every eventuality. Whatever the time of year she packed clothes for blizzards and heatwaves. She took her fur-lined boots, because nothing was worse that cold feet, and her best polyester two-piece in case she went anywhere nice. She had not so far taken her best hat in case she was introduced to the Queen, but would, the moment the idea occurred to her.

She took sun lotions and sandals, bedsocks and hot-water bottle. No one but herself could make a proper cup of tea, so she took her own favourite brand of teabags, sugar and dried milk in plastic bags, and the necessary equipment to brew up in her own room. Her sponge bag was crammed not only with flannel and toothpaste, but also remedies for every ill. There were pills for headaches and indigestion, and sticking plasters for blistered feet. There were creams for wasp and mosquito bites, and one the doctor had given her for a mysterious red patch that had once appeared on the bridge of her nose, and might pounce again, at any time.

Her leisure moments were catered for by a stock of Mills & Boon titles and quantities of wool, pins and knitting patterns. It was lucky, as Mr Bagthorpe pointed out, that her hobby was not pokerwork, or sculpture.

Mrs Fosdyke had an unshakeable conviction that her house was on the hit list of all burglars. She hid some of her less portable possessions in the coal house, but other prized articles went with her. These included framed photographs of herself with certain culinary triumphs, a cut-glass decanter given as a wedding present, and a bedside clock of enormous size and antiquity without whose ticking, she claimed, she could not sleep.

Given all this, her panic at the prospect of packing and leaving within the hour was understandable.

'I 'aven't made a list!' she shrieked again, rightly supposing that her audience was not taking this omission seriously. ' 'Ow do I know what I'll want? 'Ow do I know what to take if I don't know where I'm going and 'ow long? It could be Timbuctoo for all I know!'

Ms Page assured her that it was nowhere so exotic.

'You're going to a place that's got everything,' she said.

'Phone, telly, central heating – the lot.'

'It ain't got radiators that 'um?' demanded Mrs Fosdyke suspiciously.

'I beg your – ?'

'If it 'as, I shan't stop.'

She had once stayed in a guest house where the radiators, she claimed, had hummed, morning, noon and night. In between humming, they had made cracking noises.

'It's a great place, honestly, you'll love it,' the reporter said. 'And anything you need, we'll get it for you.'

'Anything?'

'Anything.'

Mrs Fosdyke nodded, and scurried from the room to start concertinaing a fortnight's packing into one hour.

'Why so keen on the hasty exit, Mrs Bagthorpe?' asked the reporter when she had gone.

'That is no concern of yours,' she replied. 'I will fulfil my side of the bargain, and I shall expect you to be out of here as soon as we are finished.'

'Right you are, then,' replied Patsy Page, somewhat huffily. She was used to doing any dictating of terms herself. 'Let's get stuck into Stella Bright, shall we? And why she's run off from home? Wonder what your clients will make of that one?'

'They will identify,' replied Mrs Bagthorpe calmly. 'They are only too well aware of the extremities of human emotion. And after this experience, I shall all the more easily identify with them.'

Patsy Page made a note of this but had no intention of using it. She began her dig for dirt.

Back at Unicorn House the younger Bagthorpes were sullenly performing their household duties. They washed the breakfast things and wiped cloths half-heartedly over surfaces.

'Our brains'll turn to water,' observed William gloomily.

'Mine won't,' Rosie told him. 'I do mental arithmetic while I'm dusting.'

'While you're what? Look at that table.'

The item in question had a broad, dust-free band where Rosie had swiped a duster across it, once.

'It's your turn to mop up the goat's puddle,' she countered.

'I think Daisy should mop up her own puddles,' he returned.

'Trust you to say that. You've always got it in for poor Daisy.'

'You'd better go up and see if she's still in bed,' he told her. 'If not, we'd better watch our backs.'

'I will, then!'

Rosie dropped the duster and flounced off. She nearly tripped over Jack, who was on his hands and knees brushing the carpet. The rest had flatly refused to perform this chore. Mr Bagthorpe had deliberately sucked up a sock in the Hoover and put it out of commission. If anyone should hand-brush carpets, it was he. Jack could see the logic of this, and was more or less in agreement, but he did not want his mother to return home and find her house in depressing squalor.

'You're an idiot, doing that,' she told him.

She went up to her room. Daisy's bed was empty. Even Rosie, who truly loved Daisy, felt a *frisson* of apprehension. She knew that within moments of waking up Daisy became bored and trotted forth looking for something to do. This would not be something straightforward, like playing with building bricks or dolls, as is usual with most four-year-olds. Daisy liked to interact with the real world. She saw the whole universe as her plaything.

Rosie set off in search of her favourite. She tried Grandma's room first.

'Have you seen Daisy?'

'No. As you can see, I am writing my memoirs.'

She had started this exercise quite recently. It had seemed a harmless enough activity to the others. When she had mentioned it Mrs Bagthorpe, in particular, had been most encouraging.

'I think it is a splendid idea,' she enthused. 'All old people should write their memoirs. It puts them in touch with their own childhood, and gives them a wonderful sense of their roots, and of continuity.'

Had she known it, Grandma had not the least intention of writing up her own childhood. She intended to skate, too, over her courtship and marriage to Grandpa. Her memoirs started the day after Mr Bagthorpe had been born. She was engaged on a full-scale hatchet job on her younger son.

Grandma had noticed a recent spate of memoirs, and this had given her the idea. The people who usually came badly out of memoirs were mothers and fathers – or both. She intended to correct this imbalance. She would show how her own life had been spoiled not by selfish or abusive parents, but by a selfish and abusive son. Mr Bagthorpe was not particularly famous, though he liked to think he was. When Grandma's memoirs were published, he would become famous as the worst son in human history, including Oedipus. She very much hoped she would still be alive to see this.

'Sorry, Grandma.' Rosie continued her search. As she went along the landing she heard a familiar voice. It was coming, puzzlingly, from her parents' room, which she knew to be empty.

'Perhaps Arry Awk's in there with her,' she thought, and cautiously pushed open the door.

Daisy was perched on the bed making a telephone call from the extension.

'An' I holded my breff the longest of anybody!' she was boasting. 'An' if I wanted I could hold it for ever and ever amen. What's your name?'

This might have seemed a curious question to the casual observer. Rosie, however, knew that Daisy was in the habit of dialling numbers at random, in the hope of raising someone to talk to. So far, she had done this only at home. Mr Bagthorpe approved the activity, which he believed could eventually bankrupt Uncle Parker. He said that she was probably raising the Speaking Clock in Zambia, or chatting for hours to someone in the Australian outback.

'No, my mummy don't know I'm phoning,' she was saying. 'My mummy's not here. I'm stopping wiv that nasty Uncle Bag, but he's not here either. An' Grandma's writing in a silly book and I can't find Billy Goat Gruff. Is oo big or lickle?'

There was a pause while the doubtless bewildered subscriber responded to this query.

'I *sound* lickle,' she said, 'but I'm not. I ever and ever so big. I got the longest legs in England.'

At present the legs in question were swinging over the side of the bed, well short of the floor.

'I might be going to be a giant when I grow up. I might have seven-league booties. I might go faster than my daddy's car.'

Rosie doubted this. She made no effort to terminate the conversation, which could be with someone in America for all she knew, and costing her father a fortune. (Mr Bagthorpe would later conduct a heated correspondence with British Telecom, denying all knowledge of calls made to Greenland, New Zealand and South Africa.)

'When I stand up my head knocks against the ceiling,' Daisy continued, well aware that her contact had no way of checking this. 'An' I got big green eyes and long yellow teef and I can gobble people up even over the telephone.'

At this point the subscriber evidently cut short the call. There was a pause, a series of 'Hello-hello-Daisy-Parker-here', then a disgusted slamming down of the receiver.

'Silly grockle!' she muttered, and lifting the receiver again once more started tapping out a number with her chubby forefinger. The number of digits involved seemed to indicate a very long-distance call indeed. There was a short pause.

'Hello hello!' squealed the delighted Daisy. (This was her fifth successful call to date.) 'It's Daisy Parker – who dat?'

A brief pause.

'Oh, not anybody in partickler. I jus' want a talker. You're a talker.'

She was presumably talking to a secretary of the sort whose boss is always in a meeting, or to a doctor's receptionist in some far-flung English-speaking outpost. Rosie wondered briefly how Daisy reacted when she raised, as she sometimes must by the law of averages, a Chinese or Turkish talker.

'I'se in Auntie Bag's bedroom,' she now confided, presumably in response to a question about where she was calling from. 'No, she not here. She gone missing. Billy Goat Gruff gone missing as well. And dat Mr Toole. What's your name?'

A pause.

'Dat's a funny name. Is you a witch? I been to see a witch wiv Grandma Bag, but she din't live in no gingerbread house. Is *you* in a gingerbread house?'

A pause.

'It's a rude question Mrs Fozzy says. I asked her dat and she was ever so cross. How old's you? Forty-*four*? Oooh – dat's old! You'll soon be dead!'

Daisy then went on to put in an offer for the undertaking arrangements. She listed her past burials. These included dead hamsters, little dead lambs and piggiwigs, and must have given her listener the impression that she operated from an abattoir, rather than a funeral parlour.

'You can have a bell ringing, if you like,' she concluded. 'Rosie'll ring her bell. I like Rosie.'

Her other listener glowed at this unsolicited tribute.

'No, my mummy don't know I'm phoning,' said Daisy. 'My mummy don't care. My mummy lets me do anyfing. Oh no, I mustn't take sweeties from strangers. We going to have a lickle stranger.'

66

Had she known it, the Parkers were now in line for two lickle strangers.

'Is *oo* a stranger?' To date Daisy had not quite grasped the concept of a stranger, despite Grandma's best efforts. 'Any case, you can't send sweeties on the telephone. But you better look out, 'cos I might send a death ray!'

This threat must have come out of some dim memory Daisy had of a phone call once made to her by Jack.

'I can send a death ray on the telephone an' exterminate you,' Daisy went on. 'In't it exciting? How will I know if oo's dead or not?'

A pause.

'No, I not *'tending* to be lickle, I *is* lickle. I's so lickle you can hardly see me! I'se the licklest person in the whole world!'

This, given her claims during the previous call, did seem to indicate signs of the schizophrenia Mr Bagthorpe always maintained she was suffering from.

'I'se lickler than Arry Awk and dat silly Tom Fum. I'se lickler than a milk bockle, I'se lickler dan a Mars bar and I'se lickler than a *bumble-bee!*'

She ended the litany on a triumphant note. One could only guess at the bewilderment of whoever was on the other end of the line.

'I write pomes, I write dem on walls an' I writed one about bees. I'll tell it to you. 'All the beeeezzzzz are dead!'

A pause. A click.

'*Annunner* silly grockle!' said Daisy in disgust. She replaced her own receiver, lifted it again, then started tapping out another number.

Six

In normal circumstances Mrs Bagthorpe would have been aghast at the thought of Mrs Fosdyke being whipped off to a secret address for an indefinite period. That lady, for all her shortcomings, was vital to the smooth running of the Bagthorpe household.

'She is my right arm,' she would declare, on the frequent occasions when Mr Bagthorpe wanted to sack her. 'Without her Stella Bright could never exist. And Stella Bright brings comfort to thousands. There is a certain sense in which Mrs Fosdyke brings that comfort.'

This made Mrs Fosdyke sound like a saint, rather, and Mr Bagthorpe would fiercely contend it. He would not even put Mrs Fosdyke and the word 'comfort' in the same sentence, he said. It was a contradiction in terms.

Be that as it might, on this occasion Mrs Bagthorpe felt no qualms at her employee's sudden defection. She even went up and helped with the packing. She found Mrs Fosdyke apparently attempting to cram the entire contents of her wardrobe (and much else besides) into two suitcases.

'It's 'opeless!' she said frantically. 'And if I don't take the green spotted, I shall need it, I know I shall! And there'll be no room for these!' She desperately indicated her fur-lined boots. 'I shall 'ave to wear 'em going – I'm not going without them!'

Mrs Bagthorpe wisely refrained from pointing out the

unlikelihood of a snowstorm in August. She had more than once ferried Mrs Fosdyke to the station during a heatwave, and on each occasion she had been wearing boots. These were calf-length and unwieldy, and would have occupied a lot of room in any suitcase.

'Could you not just carry them separately?' Mrs Bagthorpe suggested. 'After all, you will be travelling by car.'

'What – and leave 'em on the back seat?' shrieked Mrs Fosdyke. 'I'd best put 'em on now, while I remember. Ooh, I don't know if I'm doing the right thing going!'

'Of course you are, dear,' Mrs Bagthorpe assured her. 'And you are not to worry about how the rest of us will cope.'

Mrs Fosdyke had not in fact given this a second thought.

'There'll be a chauffeur,' she said. 'Imagine! Just like the Queen! Ooh, I wish I'd 'ad me 'air done!'

'Your hair looks perfectly lovely,' her employer told her. She lowered her voice. 'And, Gladys dear, you are not to worry about Max.'

She had not given him a second thought, either, except to pray that he would not be discovered, and spoil her chances.

'The main thing,' Mrs Bagthorpe continued in a whisper, 'is to say nothing. Careless words cost lives.'

'Ooh, 'e'll never be 'anged, will 'e?'

'Of course not. But you must guard against careless talk.'

'I ain't very good at fibbing,' Mrs Fosdyke confided, remembering the earlier postcard episode.

'Simply keep telling yourself you have not seen Max for years,' Mrs Bagthorpe advised. 'It is, after all, almost true. If you keep repeating it silently to yourself, your subconscious mind will come to believe it. Then, if anyone asks about him, you will not be caught off guard.'

All this was Greek to Mrs Fosdyke, who knew nothing about the subconscious mind, and would certainly have had no truck with it even if she had. However, she did dimly grasp the gist of what was said, and clutched at this straw.

'I ain't seen Max for years, I ain't seen Max for years,' she muttered as she fished a bag of hair rollers from a drawer. 'I ain't seem 'im with 'is 'orrible long 'air, and Lord knows I don't know anything about 'im robbing cash cards.'

'Only in desperation,' Mrs Bagthorpe reminded her. 'He is as prone to human failings as any of us. I shall set him back upon the right path.'

Mrs Fosdyke was not even listening, busy as she was bundling her alarm clock into thick-knit stockings, and stowing it in the case.

'At least I shan't sleep over. I ain't seen Max for years. At least I shall 'ear it ticking, and it'll seem like 'ome. I ain't seen Max for years. 'Ooever would've thought 'e'd turn out like that? Lovely 'e was, when 'e was a baby.'

'Just keep trying to *think* of him as a baby,' suggested Mrs Bagthorpe unnecessarily.

'Ready up there?' came the voice of Patsy Page.

'She mustn't come up!' hissed Mrs Bagthorpe. 'Ready!' she carolled.

Mrs Fosdyke began frantically trying to close the lid.

'Someone'll 'ave to fetch 'em down! I can't lift 'em!'

'Leave it to me!'

Mrs Bagthorpe went hastily along the landing and tapped on Max's door.

' 'Oo is it?' came a whisper.

'Me!' She opened the door and put her head round. Max was seated on his bed, dejectedly staring ahead at the trophies of his childhood.

'You must get under the bed,' she hissed, 'or in the wardrobe, in case someone looks in!'

He needed no prompting. He was under the bed in a flash.

'I'll tell you when it's all clear!'

She softly closed the door and went downstairs. There she

70

found a uniformed chauffeur in conference with Ms Page.

'Perhaps Mrs Fosdyke's bags can be brought down now?' she said.

'I'll just nip up and use the facilities.' Ms Page followed the chauffeur out. Mrs Bagthorpe winced. She was well aware of the thoroughness of any *Sludge* reporter, and prayed that this did not extend to looking under the beds.

Mrs Fosdyke descended, quite pink with pleasure. Never before had a uniformed chauffeur carried her bags. Within moments Ms Page reappeared.

'Took a peek into Max's room,' she said, making a mental note to get it photographed.

'I ain't seen Max for years,' said Mrs Fosdyke.

'Now – are we ready for the off? Got everything?'

'For years and years,' said Mrs Fosdyke.

'Quick as you can into the car, Mrs Fosdyke, and try to keep your head down.'

'Head down? They'll never be shooting, will they?' By this she meant terrorists, rather than the press corps.

'They'll try,' said Ms Page, misunderstanding her. 'You don't want all that unwelcome publicity. Perhaps you should put that over your head.' She indicated the plastic raincoat over Mrs Fosdyke's arm. That lady took up the suggestion with alacrity.

''Ere!' came her muffled voice. ' 'Oo's locking up after us?'

'You can leave that to me,' said Mrs Bagthorpe hastily. 'I have a key, remember.'

'The key's in the grill pan,' came the muffled voice. 'I ain't seen Max for years.'

'Of course you haven't,' said Patsy Page soothingly. Her first priority, she by now realized, was to put a trace on the missing Max. 'Off we go now! Fame and fortune, remember, Mrs F!'

And so Mrs Fosdyke left her home on her way to fame and fortune, fur-lined boots protruding under her turquoise two-piece, and a plastic mac draped over her head. A buzz ran through the assembled paparazzi, bulbs fizzed and popped.

'Come on – give us a smile!' they pleaded, and called her name, 'Gladys – Gladys, love – over here!'

But Mrs Fosdyke was under contract to the *Sludge*, and had Patsy Page as minder. She was steered swiftly toward the waiting car and unceremoniously bundled in. The plastic mac was pulled free in the process. The last view Mrs Bagthorpe had of her was her sitting proudly, hat by now seriously askew, slowly waving her hand in the manner of the Queen Mother. Photographers ran alongside, jostling for position. Others ran to their cars and started them up and set off in pursuit. Within two minutes Coldharbour Road was deserted.

Mrs Bagthorpe dropped the net curtain and let out a long sigh of relief. The way of escape was now open. Max's rehabilitation could begin.

Uncle Parker and Mr Bagthorpe spent the taxi ride into Aysham engaged in sporadic verbal sparring. Uncle Parker made frequent reference to the disappearance of Mrs Bagthorpe, and in particular the unsavoury publicity this was bound to engender, and the possibility of Mr Bagthorpe ending up in prison.

'Though, let's face it, you can write your scripts anywhere. Oscar Wilde did, and Bunyan. And you could pick up some good material.'

Mr Bagthorpe reminded him that Daisy was still at Unicorn House, doubtless wreaking havoc, and running up another enormous bill. He challenged Uncle Parker to cough up for the slaughtered goldfish, but he politely declined, saying that the matter was still *sub judice*.

It was a relief to arrive in Aysham, where a smattering of reporters still hung around the police station. The pair climbed out of the taxi and were photographed, in case they turned out to be relatives of the Knaresborough Knifer.

72

Both had to pay up to retrieve their vehicles from the police pound, and both were warned that there could be charges. Then each went his separate way.

Uncle Parker toyed with the idea of searching for Mr O'Toole, but decided that he had probably now been displaced in his wife's affections by the Green-Eyed Angel. Instead, he made for Interior Design, where he requested that someone should urgently come out to The Knoll with pattern books and samples. There was no trouble at all about this. Uncle Parker was a highly valued customer. No one else on the books changed décor with such frequency, or at such expense. This was partly due to the activities of Daisy and Billy Goat Gruff, and partly to Aunt Celia herself. She changed her décor as most people change socks. Now that she had had a visitation by an angel, there were bound to be changes. There would probably be a lot of cherubs, and ceilings in the manner of the Sistine Chapel.

'But madam has already chosen the refurbishments for the nursery, sir,' an assistant felt bound to point out.

'Scrub it,' he told her. 'There've been developments.'

By this he meant the glass-smashing session of the goat, and the expectation of two little strangers rather than one. He could not help wondering how long his wife's Phantom Pregnancy would last. The doctors certainly seemed to have no idea. The only comfort was that it would not culminate in the eventual appearance of another brace of Daisys.

Mr Bagthorpe had already worked out his own plan. There was absolutely no point in returning to Unicorn House, which now contained only his parents and his children (plus, of course, Daisy Parker and her goat). Without his wife and Mrs Fosdyke things would, he realized, go rapidly downhill.

'I shall not be able to write a word,' he told himself. 'And I owe it to the nation to go on writing. I could go and stay in a hotel like Jeffrey Archer does.'

This was not such an attractive proposition as it seemed

because Mr Bagthorpe detested hotels, however grand. He maintained that a hotel was habitable in inverse ratio to the number of stars or rosettes it boasted.

'The more stars, the more booby-traps,' he would say. He knew this because he sometimes stayed in such hotels when attending conferences, and always came home saying it had been a nightmare.

'It was like trying to sleep in a Turkish bath.' One of his most common complaints was that such places were invariably overheated. The windows would not open, and the knobs on the radiators were stuck.

His real hate was the bedside clock radio. Mr Bagthorpe had never mastered the workings of such a device, and had a paranoid conviction that even if left severely alone, it would leap into life at two a.m. playing New Orleans jazz. On the one occasion he had attempted to set it, the alarm had sounded, and he could not work out how to turn it off. He had stuck lavatory paper in his ears and tried to get to sleep. He pulled the covers over his ears and lay there stifled and fuming. In the end he had rung down to reception, and a supercilious night porter had come up and flicked a switch.

'Oh, it's that one, is it?' Mr Bagthorpe had said. 'I was not trained as an electronics engineer.'

'It's quite simple, sir,' the porter had told him. 'Most other guests welcome the facility. See!'

He had set the alarm again, then demonstrated how to switch it off.

'Easy!' he had said.

'Flying a jet plane is easy,' Mr Bagthorpe had told him, 'once you've got all the knobs and dials sorted.'

When the porter had gone Mr Bagthorpe had ill-advisedly attempted to reset the alarm himself, while the instructions were still fresh in his mind. He had, after all, by now already lost quite a lot of sleep, and might need rousing. The results were as before. This time he was well and truly stymied. He could not bear the loss of face involved in calling back the porter. He spent the night brewing endless cups of tea and coffee.

'And even then I had to fill the kettle from the bath tap!' he had told his unsympathetic family. 'Four stars – and filling your kettle from the bath like any dosser!'

'Why didn't you just pull the plug, Father?' asked Rosie.

'Pull the what?'

'On the radio. Just pull it out of the socket.'

Mr Bagthorpe was not a practical man, and this simple expedient had just never occurred to him. Now, his first action on arrival in a hotel room was to get down on his hands and knees and crawl around following electric leads, to track down the plug to the clock radio. Sometimes this involved moving beds. Sometimes, in the more up-to-date hotels, there were no plugs. Everything electrical was operated by an incomprehensible panel set into the bedside table. It was all Mr Bagthorpe could do to locate the reading light, let alone the clock. This sort of hotel usually had a gymnasium, sports complex and swimming pool, all of which were anathema to him.

'I visit a hotel for a night's sleep, not in order to train for the Olympics,' he would say.

At breakfast he would glower over his eggs, bacon, sausage, black pudding, mushrooms and tomatoes at the freshly exercised and showered executives who were spooning up their grapefruit and mucsli.

Given all this, a couple of nights in a hotel was not the attractive prospect it might seem to most people. He was used to better food at home than most hotels serve up, and there was no one to shout at. However, the provider of the superior meals would probably not report for duty in the foreseeable future, and home became automatically a threatening milieu when Daisy and her goat were in residence.

Mr Bagthorpe plumped for a hotel. He did not, however,

select an attractive location a good distance from home. He felt threatened in strange environments, though naturally did not admit this. His unease took the form of severe criticism of whatever place he found himself in. Thus the Cotswolds became 'Toytown', and Wales 'a sheep-infested backwater'.

He decided that there was no reason why he should not book into a hotel in Aysham itself.

'Oh, just a couple of nights,' he told the receptionist, when asked about the length of his stay. 'It depends which way the cookie crumbles.'

This was an odd sort of reply. The receptionist noted that he appeared to have no baggage. She had been alerted to this kind of customer who appears without baggage and then departs early – without payment. She pushed forward a form.

'Perhaps you could fill this in for me, sir.'

'I am checking into the hotel, not applying for a post as bottle-washer,' he returned.

'Just a formality,' she said.

Mr Bagthorpe knew this perfectly well. He had filled in numerous such forms in the past, though with an ill grace. His handwriting was wellnigh illegible at the best of times. On these occasions he produced the kind of scrawl any doctor would have been proud of. He objected to forms on principle. He believed they were all fed into computers, and filed by some kind of sinister Big Brother.

'The government will soon know the colour of my socks,' he would say, 'and the brand of my toothpaste.'

He made his usual scribbled entries and pushed the paper back.

'Thank you, Mr . . . Mr . . .' The receptionist peered. 'Rathbones . . .? Bilsthorpe . . . Beanpole . . .?

'Bagthorpe!' snapped the visitor.

'Er – you don't appear to have filled in your car registration number, sir.'

76

Mr Bagthorpe groaned.

'Don't you start,' he said. 'Would you believe I was arrested yesterday for not knowing it?'

The receptionist's eyes widened. She was an avid watcher of *Crimewatch UK*, and yearned to be able to make a call to their incident room.

'By the police?'

'Of course by the police! Numskulled idiots!'

'Height around six feet,' the receptionist was mentally noting. 'Hair brown and scruffy . . . eyes blue . . . shabby green corduroy jacket . . .'

'Look, are you going to give me my key, or aren't you?'

The receptionist thought fast. If she insisted on the car registration number, the suspect might panic and leave. Her best course was to check him in and let him go up to his room. This would then be covered with his fingerprints. Also, she could note his movements if he came and went, and their exact times. Mr Bagthorpe looked exactly the type to rob a building society, she thought, using the Crown and Mitre as base.

'Here is your key, sir.' She lifted it gingerly from its hook so that it would bear his fingerprints rather than her own, and passed it over. 'Would you like someone to help you with your baggage?'

'What baggage?' he returned. 'I carry my own baggage inside my own head.'

No client of the Crown and Mitre had ever made such a statement before. The receptionist was made quite nervous by it. This man could be mad, as well as criminal.

'Of course, sir,' she agreed feebly. 'Take the lift to the second floor and turn first left, sir. I hope you enjoy your stay, sir.'

'There's no need to "sir" me in every breath,' he told her. 'It cuts no ice with me.'

'No, sir.' The receptionist had rather hoped it would. It had occurred to her that he might be out to rob the hotel, rather than a building society, and she was right beside the safe.

Mr Bagthorpe followed her directions and found his room. He entered it warily.

'Usual fug,' he said to himself, and his eyes went straight to the windows. 'Oh my God. Usual set-up.'

He would be at the mercy of the hotel's thermostats and air conditioning for the duration of his stay. Mr Bagthorpe hated to be at the mercy of anyone or anything. His inclination was either to smash the glass or bolt. But Unicorn House, though at least its windows opened, was currently hugely unappealing. He was trapped.

He spent the next few minutes on his hands and knees tracking down the plug for the radio alarm. He pulled it, and felt better. Then he entered the bathroom.

'Dammit!' he exclaimed. 'I haven't got 'em with me!'

By this, he meant the small bars of soap and bottles of bath oil, shampoo and so forth, tastefully marked with the name and logo of the hotel, and meant as enticing freebies for the visitor. Mr Bagthorpe held these in the utmost contempt.

'Sewing kits, for crying out loud!' he would say. 'Do they think I've gone there to sit and sew on buttons? Almond bath essence! If I wanted almonds in my bath, I'd chuck 'em in myself. What kind of person wants to go round smelling of marzipan?'

Mr Bagthorpe had gone through several manoeuvres over the years to demonstrate his contempt to the management. At first he had contented himself with opening every bar of soap and using it, and tipping out the contents of every single bottle in sight. It then occurred to him that the management might think he had actually used these products. On the other hand, if he simply removed them, he would be thought the kind of person who treasured such pathetic items, and took them home to use, or to give as stocking-fillers.

He had then hit upon a very neat scheme. He would carefully

collect the matches, sewing kit, soap, bath essence and shampoo, all bearing the name and logo of the Queen's Head, Wolverhampton, say. These he kept in his overnight bag. Then, on his next visit to a hotel, to the Flying Duck, Frinton, say, he would carefully remove all *their* freebies, and replace them with those from the Queen's Head. He was delighted with this ploy.

'That'll show 'em what I think of their tawdry bribes,' he would say. 'If they've got money to spare to buy bath gel, let 'em send it to Oxfam.'

On this occasion Mr Bagthorpe did not have his bag with him, complete with toiletries courtesy of the Bear Inn, Bournemouth. Nor, for that matter, did he even have his own toothbrush. He was already sick of his room, and grateful for an excuse to leave it. He set off for a shopping expedition to the High Street. The manager and the receptionist were in conference as he crossed the lobby.

'Look! That's him!'

The manager, who was in his first posting, acted swiftly.

'I'll hold the fort here. You nip round to the back and watch the car park. If we get his car number, that'll be a start.

They had already decided that Mr Bagthorpe had probably checked in under a false name.

'What kind of person is called Handbag?' the receptionist had asked. She had been so flustered at the time that she now genuinely believed that this was the name he had given.

The guest went blithely on, unaware that he was under surveillance.

'Might as well do it now I'm here, I s'pose,' he thought, and headed for the car park. The receptionist, positioned behind net curtains at the rear of the building, saw the suspect Mr Handbag appear and head purposefully across the yard. She watched, notepad and pen poised . . .

Seven

'I'll do it!' said Rosie.

'No, I will,' said Tess.

'*I'll* do it,' said William. 'I'm eldest. And don't come any sexist rot about it being a girl's job. Mother's trying to crack down on that. And all the top chefs in the world are men.'

'Delia Smith isn't.'

'Exception that proves the rule. Any case, she's not a chef. She just cooks things up on the telly and sells books of recipes.'

'Which I'm using,' put in Tess.

They were arguing about who was to be cook for the day. All three were hell-bent on adding *haute cuisine* as a String to their Bows. As yet, none of them knew even the basics. All they knew was how to stick Smarties on to iced buns and do a good fry-up. Mrs Fosdyke had always jealously guarded the kitchen as her exclusive territory. Even the fry-ups had been achieved in her absence.

Every cookery book in the house was out and lying on the kitchen table. Elaborate menus were being concocted.

'I'm not bothered about doing it,' Jack said. 'I don't think I'd be much good at it.'

No one troubled to respond. They had already taken this as read.

'I'm doing chicken liver and brandy pâté for lunch,' Tess said.

'Oh yes?' said William. 'What are you going to use for chicken livers?'

'And brandy,' Rosie chipped in. 'The goldfish drank all the brandy.'

'And salmon mousse followed by duck in redcurrant sauce tonight,' Tess continued.

'Going to fish a salmon out of the Dead Sea, are you?' William asked.

Jack and Rosie tittered. Tess glowered at them. She realized that they were right. Such ingredients were not to be found at the village shop, which ran only to such basics as fish fingers and oxtail soup.

'I shall inspect the contents of the pantry and deep freeze and adjust my menu accordingly,' she said.

'Hey – that's a thought!' Jack said, brightening. I bet there's some of Fozzy's stuff in the deep freeze – she nearly always does some extra to freeze.'

All three rounded on him.

'I don't think you're quite getting the point,' William told him.

'Anything Fozzy can cook, I can cook,' Tess said.

'And me! I'm going to be top cook in the world.'

'You can't all do it,' Jack told them. 'Not all at once. Too many cooks spoil the broth.'

'Thank you, Mastermind,' William said. 'We're not all doing it. I am.'

'No, *I* am!'

The wrangling started again. Jack went out and left them to it, and Zero slunk after him. He always got low to the ground when voices were raised – which was often.

'Don't worry, old chap,' Jack told him. 'You'll be all right. There's plenty of tins of your meat, and a stack of Buried Bones.' (Zero had won himself a lifetime's supply of Buried Bones during his career in advertising.)

'Mind you, I'll probably end up eating them myself.'

81

Jack was not hopeful about the chances of his siblings achieving *cordon bleu* status at a stroke. He had sometimes watched Mrs Fosdyke when she was cooking, and without ever actually putting the thought into words, had noticed that she seemed almost to become another person. At other times she scuttled and banged. Once she had started creating a dish her movements – even her expression – altered. She swooped and dived, her fingers flew like those of a concert pianist. Her recipe book, stained and floury, sometimes lay open on the table, but she hardly seemed to glance at it. She would sometimes juggle three or four dishes at the same time, moving deftly from one to another, stirring, tasting, opening and shutting the oven, in a dance that seemed at the time both free and choreographed.

'They might think they're geniuses,' Jack thought, 'but I bet they can't cook.'

By now he had reached the stile that led into the meadow. He wondered whether he should extend his search for his mother.

'Someone in Passingham might have seen her.'

He looked over towards the village and, incredibly, there she was, a familiar, higgledy-piggledy figure with her flapping skirts and fly-away hair. Jack let out a whoop of joy.

'Mother!'

He was over the stile and racing to meet her, and then caught and hugged her as if he were six years old again and running to her with a cut knee.

'Oh Mother, you're safe! I thought – ' He did not know what he thought, but felt the silly tears spring to his eyes, and rubbed them surreptitiously with her floating smock.

'Oh Jack, you silly boy, dear boy!' And Mrs Bagthorpe felt her own eyes fill. The previous day she had fled from a home that seemed cold and filled with a family of strangers. Now she was returning, uncertain of her welcome, and was being greeted like the prodigal son. At her feet Zero wagged and pranced and nudged his nose.

'Zero, dear old boy!' she cried.

Jack emerged from her embrace. As he sped towards his mother he had dimly registered that she was not alone, and now, for the first time, he really saw her companion. It was no one he recognized, and could easily have been a relative or colleague of Mr O'Toole.

'Someone with a Problem she's picked up,' he thought, and tried not to stare.

'Oh Jack, it's lovely to see you!' She felt as if she had been away for a month. 'Oh – and do you remember Max?'

Max! Beneath the tangled hair Jack could see the pale weasel face of Mrs Fosdyke's missing son.

'Oh – of course. How are you?'

'He's going to be perfectly splendid, aren't you, Max?'

Mrs Bagthorpe took an arm of each and began to propel them along with her.

'I have taken him under my wing.'

That, Jack realized, was exactly right. His mother was exactly like a mother hen. With her ample form and wide, flapping sleeves like wings, she even looked like one.

'That's nice,' he said, and meant it. His mother was home, and the whole world was nice. 'Who cares what's for dinner?'

'What, dear?'

'Nothing.'

'Oh, such a lot has happened – I can hardly begin to tell you. But the main thing, for now, is that Max is coming to stay.'

'What? With us?' Jack was bewildered. He knew that Max's mother had gone off to a safe house or bungalow, but had assumed that her own house was still there.

'I'll explain all later. Now, how is everyone?'

Most people would not bother asking this, after an absence of only twenty-four hours. Mrs Bagthorpe knew all too well what a difference a day makes.

'That lot are all fighting over who cooks. They want to be Cordon Blues.'

'Oh, I see. In Mrs Fosdyke's absence. That's all very exciting.' Her Positive Thinking was to the fore again.

'Daisy and the goat are there as well – at least, they were last night.' He felt a flicker of unease as he remembered that neither, so far as he knew, had been sighted that morning.

'Father's gone into Aysham with Uncle Park to get their cars back.'

'To what, dear?'

Jack filled her in. He told her of his father's arrest, and how Uncle Parker had bailed him out.

'It'll all be in the papers,' he told her. 'It was on telly – *and* about Fozzy's bomb – *and* about you being a Missing Person.'

Mrs Bagthorpe stopped in her tracks.

'What?'

She was aghast. Despite her husband's and Grandma's accusations of attention-seeking, it had never crossed her mind that, in disappearing in order to gather herself together, she would become officially Missing. Indeed, in so far as she had thought about it, she had believed (rightly) that she would hardly be missed at all.

'The police made me find a photo of you, but it wasn't a very good one,' Jack said. 'In the garden, wearing one of Grandpa's hats.'

Mrs Bagthorpe shuddered, Mercifully, she did not remember seeing this on Mrs Fosdyke's screen. At the time she had still been in the zombie-like trance induced by the contemplation of yet another sucked-up sock.

'Grandma thought you were in Harrogate,' he went on.

'Harrogate? Why ever would I go there?'

'I don't know,' he admitted. 'Something to do with Agatha Christie.'

'Oh. I see.' She began to feel a certain healthy indignation.

84

'So that's what they thought, is it?'

'So where were you?' he asked.

'At Mrs Fosdyke's house, of course.'

'So why didn't you ring and – ' he broke off. Mrs Fosdyke had no phone. 'I was nearly going spare.'

'I'm sorry, Jack.'

'And the house was full of police.'

It was now Max's turn to stop in his tracks. Unicorn House never looked much like a safe haven to him. If it was overrun with pigs, it was a no-go area.

'I reckon I'd best do a runner,' he said.

'No, Max,' said Mrs Bagthorpe firmly. 'That is the last thing to do for someone in your position.'

'Done it before,' he said sullenly.

'I know – but do you wish that to be the pattern of your life? Hounded from pillar to post, always afraid of recognition, your crime hanging over you like the Sword of Damocles?'

Max had not a clue what the Sword of Damocles was.

'Done it before,' he said again.

'We are going to change all that,' she told him. 'We are going to turn your whole life around. Do you trust me, Max?'

He looked at her eager, flushed face and did, rather.

'But the pigs are in there!' he protested.

'Listen. You shall stay outside – in the shed, if you like. I will go in first and assess the situation.'

Jack had not the least idea what they were talking about, but was beginning to guess. He wondered what crime Max had committed. They were now at the stile that led into the garden. His mother stepped up and over, then turned.

'Come along, Max,' she said. 'Up you go. Think of it as the first step into a glorious new future.'

'After you,' Jack said.

Max hesitated, then swung over the fence.

'There!' she cried. 'That was not so hard, was it?'

85

The trio went through the shrubbery and towards the vegetable garden, where the shed stood.

'Hsst!' hissed Max, and tugged at Mrs Bagthorpe's sleeve. They listened. Someone else was in the garden. Jack knew at once who it was.

'Now what's she up to?' he said.

'Oh dear!' Mrs Bagthorpe's world was beginning to close in on her again. 'Perhaps we had better look.'

'One two free four five
 Once I caught a fishy live!'

'The pool!' gasped Mrs Bagthorpe. 'She might fall in!'

'And she might be pushed,' thought Jack grimly.

''Cept dey's not live. Dey's dead. Dey an't got no lickle legs but dey's dead anyway.'

Now they could see her. Daisy was crouching by the Dead Sea, wielding a large saucepan. Beside her was a dinner plate. On it lay a bloated, probably smelly, fish.

'Oo shall have a fishy
 On a lickle dishy!'

Daisy carolled, and swept the saucepan through the curdled water as she sang. Plop! Another fish dropped on to the plate.

'Pooh – what a sniffy!' She wrinkled her nose. 'Never mind. You's going to play wiv der poor lickle dead sheep and hens.

'Why did you let him go?
 'Cos he bit my finger so.'

Plop! Another fish. All of a sudden she laid down the dripping saucepan.

'I'se hungry,' she announced. She had been up ages, and missed breakfast by making long-distance telephone calls, among other things. She gazed thoughtfully at the landed fish.

'She's never going to eat them!' Jack watched in horrified fascination. Daisy was an original, all right, but he had never so far thought of her as ghoulish, even during her Funeral Holding Phase.

'You jus' wait here,' she told the fish. 'I'se jus' going to have a runny egg wiv soldiers.'

'She'll be lucky,' Jack thought. 'I bet that lot've polished off the eggs.'

'An' den we'll have a lovely funeral wiv hymns,' Daisy continued. 'We'll have *All Fings Bright and Bootiful*, all fishies great and small. You'll like dat.'

She skipped off towards the house.

'Oh dear,' murmured Mrs Bagthorpe. 'Daisy really is trying. She really shouldn't be playing alone by water, at her age.'

'Those fish don't look exactly hygienic,' Jack said. 'They look as if they're going to explode.'

'Oh dear! I'd better go after her, and make sure she washes her hands before breakfast.'

'Daisy never washes her hands,' Jack told her. 'She's survived till now. She never washes her neck, either. You ought to see it.'

'At her age, it is really her mother who is responsible for her neck,' said Mrs Bagthorpe, who in her time had been an assiduous scrubber of that part of her own children's anatomy. 'But dear Celia seems entirely taken up with the new arrival.'

Jack did not feel that this was the right moment to tell her that the new arrival had now doubled up to twins, and that they were Phantom, anyway. In any case, he had not yet fully grasped exactly what *was* going on. It had not seemed to square with what he had so far learned in biology about human reproduction.

The trio moved on, and as they reached the vegetable garden Max stopped again.

'I could 'ide in there.' He jerked his head towards the potting-shed.

'There is absolutely no need for that,' said Mrs Bagthorpe firmly. 'There is plenty of room in the house.'

'Just while you sus things out.'

He was already making for the shed.

'But, Max, there is no need to hide in there. If anyone sees you, they'll think you are the gardener. If you hide – '

'Eeeowch!'

Things happened at the speed of light. Max threw open the door of the shed and Billy Goat Gruff ran out and butted him square in the stomach. Max howled and doubled up, clutching himself. The goat stood for a moment rolling his yellow eyes, made a half-run at Jack, then veered off and disappeared among the bushes.

Jack went forward, and saw that Billy Goat Gruff had not sat around wasting time while shut in the shed. Its contents were shattered, spilt and piled in heaps.

'But how did he get in there?' he wondered.

It later emerged that between dialling New Zealand and panning for dead goldfish, Daisy had played at prisons. There had been much talk of them the previous day, and none of this had escaped her sharp ears. She knew for a fact that Uncle Bag was in there, and had heard Grandma say that they should lock the door and throw away the key. Also, Daisy knew her fairy-tales inside out, and there was quite a lot of locking up in those, too.

She had fixed on her pet as a suitable candidate for internment, and gone in search of him. He had in fact spent the night outside. In Mrs Bagthorpe's absence no one had bothered to lock, or even shut, doors and windows. If the Knaresborough Knifer *had* been in the vicinity, he could have had a field day.

Daisy found the goat polishing off a row of lettuce, and had led him unprotesting towards the shed, which had seemed a suitable prison.

'It's all dark and spidery, like a dudgeon. You's a bad boy and you're going to prison,' she told him severely. 'You might be der for years and years and years. An' you'll eat bread and water and be sorry for all the fings you've done wrong.'

This, in the case of Billy Goat Gruff, would have been a very comprehensive catalogue. Daisy told him all this in the hopes that he might put up some kind of fight. He was disappointingly docile for one being threatened with years of incarceration.

'It's horrid in prison wiv spiders and all water dripping,' she continued. Still he ambled peacefully beside her. She did not even have to tug at his satin halter.

'An' sometimes you get torchered wiv screws,' she went on. 'I might come and torcher you later if der's time. *Der!*'

She gave the goat a push into the shed and slammed the door. She was disappointed to find there was no key to turn and throw away.

'You can't open no doors anyway, 'cos you an't got no fingers!' she called. 'You jus' stop there and be sorry!'

Again, reaction had been nil. The goat was full of lettuce and therefore, like Peter Rabbit, soporific. Only later, after a doze, had his fight returned.

Jack and his mother only learned this later, but could already guess at most of it.

'You see that?' demanded the incredulous Max. 'A goat!'

'It is Daisy's pet, and quite harmless,' said Mrs Bagthorpe.

''Armless?' repeated Max, still clutching himself. ''Armless?'

'He merely ran out and you happened to be in the way,' she said, manufacturing evidence.

'And look at it in there!' He peered in at his proposed hide-out.

'I don't think you should hide,' she told him again. 'Your self-esteem will suffer if you think of yourself as someone who has to skulk in corners.'

Max cared not a fig for his self-esteem. His instinct was to hide.

'Tell you what,' he said. ''Ow about I stay 'ere and tidy this lot up 'while you sus things out?'

Mrs Bagthorpe hesitated.

'That is very kind of you,' she said. 'But I shall have to ask you to give your word that you will not run off.'

'Run off? Where to?' said Max bitterly. Certainly not home.

'Then you give your word?'

'Yeah. Yeah – for what it's worf.'

Jack himself thought the wording of this guarantee decidedly dodgy, but his mother seemed to accept it. She did, however, display a certain cunning.

'You must be hungry, Max,' she said. 'As soon as possible I shall arrange for food.'

'I could eat an 'orse,' he told her.

'I think we can do better than that,' she told him with a smile.

Jack was not so sure. He was glad to see his mother smile again, but aware that she did not yet know what she was walking back into. The deep-freeze had not yet been fully restocked since their absence in Wales. Rations were short. He looked sourly at Max, seeing in him yet another mouth to feed.

'What did you bring *him* for?' he asked as they continued towards the house. 'And why's he scared of the fuzz? What's he done?'

Mrs Bagthorpe told him. 'But any one of us might have done the same in such circumstances,' she said.

'*You* wouldn't,' Jack told her.

'There is much good in Max,' she said Positively. 'And I intend to rehabilitate him into society.'

'How?'

'He has been on the run, and away from any civilizing influence.'

She clearly believed that at Unicorn House he would find such civilizing influence. Even Jack could see that this was not the case. Max would be better off in the potting-shed.

As they approached the house they were met by the sounds of drum, fiddle and fractured Wagner.

90

'That means Tess is cooking,' Jack deduced. The other two, feeling threatened, were punishing their instruments, and Grandma was just keeping her end up.

'Oh, how lovely to be home again!' cried Mrs Bagthorpe, hurrying her steps.

In the kitchen Tess was slamming around looking vainly for ingredients.

'No eggs, no salmon, no redcurrants!'

'Tess, darling!' Mrs Bagthorpe moved towards her daughter, arms outstretched.

'Oh – you're back!' remarked her daughter, waving floury hands to fend off the embrace. 'Thank goodness for that. Do you realize we're clean out of nearly everything? There aren't even any eggs!'

'I found a 'nana,' came another voice. Jack had not at first noticed Daisy who, peeled banana in hand, was peering into the fridge.

'You'll have to go into Aysham,' Tess continued. 'I'll make a list.'

'You won't be able to,' Jack told his mother. 'Father's got the car.'

'Hell's bells!' Tess slammed her pencil down. 'Why can't we have two cars like everyone else?'

'Because your father says he can't afford it,' Mrs Bagthorpe replied, 'and because it is extremely un-Green.'

'There is no such thing as un-Green,' Tess told her. 'Either a thing is green, or it is not. The concept of *un*-Greenness – '

'Oh shut up!' Jack said. 'Aren't you even going to ask Mother where she's been?'

'Where *have* you been?' Tess asked, more in a spirit of accusation than filial concern.

'Pussy cat pussy cat where've you been? I been up to London to look at der Queen,' remarked Daisy. She had found half a loaf of bread, and plonked it on the table.

'I think you'll have to take a taxi into town,' Tess went on, without waiting for an answer. 'Father's trying to get out of doing things, as per usual. I bet anything he won't be home till tonight.'

'Ah, Laura! So there you are!'

It was Grandma who, having written a sizeable and libellous chunk of her memoirs, was also in search of food.

'Oh Mother – how lovely to see you!'

'I can hardly believe that you could behave so irresponsibly,' Grandma went on. 'A mother, to walk out and abandon her family! Poor Henry was actually suspected of doing away with you.'

'What nonsense!' returned Mrs Bagthorpe. 'Henry would not harm a fly.'

'I do not agree,' Grandma told her. 'Henry has deep, secret springs of violence. I am his mother, and should know. Great heaven – whatever is the child doing!'

She moved swiftly forward and snatched the bread knife from Daisy's hand.

'There!' she cried, brandishing it. 'That is the sort of thing that happens when mothers desert their young!'

'Mother isn't Daisy's mother,' Jack pointed out.

'I want toasty soldiers I want toasty soldiers!' Daisy screamed. Shreds of banana flew from her lips.

In the end, all anybody got was toast and marmalade. By the time they had finished it, Tess had drawn up a list filling the backs of two foolscap envelopes.

'I'll get a taxi into Aysham,' she said.

'And bring back takeaways for lunch,' Jack suggested.

'We goin' to play a game, Grandma Bag,' Daisy said.

'And what is that, Daisy dear?' Grandma inquired.

'It a secret,' replied that cherub. 'It a deep dark secret.' What she had in mind was to put Grandma in prison.

'Lovely, dear,' said Grandma vaguely.

'Oo got to come wiv me,' Daisy told her, climbing down. 'It in der garden.'

'I think I must request that it is nothing to do with goldfish,' Grandma said, allowing herself to be led away.

'Oh, it in't no goldfish,' Daisy assured her, shaking her ringlets. 'It a bigger surprise dan goldfish.'

It certainly was. Grandma was in for a very big surprise indeed. The pair of them wove their way through the sunlit garden, Daisy now thoroughly mellow at the prospect of incarcerating her grandmother.

'I already done one surprise dis morning,' she confided.

She had already cast Billy Goat Gruff into prison. Now Grandma was to join him.

Max, hearing voices, shut the potting-shed door and concealed himself under some dusty sacks in the far corner.

'Here we are.' Daisy halted. 'Dis is der surprise. You jus' go in, Grandma Bag.'

'How exciting,' murmured Grandma, opening the door and stepping cautiously inside.

'Der!' cried Daisy triumphantly. She gave Grandma a push and slammed the door behind her.

Eight

Unlike his brother-in-law, Uncle Parker saw no reason to stay
away from home for as long as possible. There lay his treasure
(albeit expecting Phantom Twins), and his daughter and her
goat were for the moment safely off the premises.

He had been genuinely alarmed by Aunt Celia's behaviour
the previous night. That weird, high wailing had been something new, and a visitation from an angel had never before been
on the agenda. The only thing he could hope for was that this
heavenly messenger had come to tell her that she was not, after
all, expecting twins.

As he passed Unicorn House he noted a large, bearded man
with a camera in discussion with another, and a couple of cars
parked near by.

'Hello,' he thought. 'Looks like the paparazzi. The start of
the siege. Poor old Henry.'

Much cheered, he sped on his way. As he approached his
own entrance he saw another couple of empty, parked cars.
Given that The Knoll was the only dwelling in sight, there
seemed little doubt where its occupants were. Unable to operate
the electronically powered gates, they had set off up the drive
on foot.

Cursing under his breath, Uncle Parker roared through the
gates and up the drive, coming to a halt in a spurt of gravel. He
leapt nimbly from the car and up the steps to the front door. As

soon as he stepped inside his fears were confirmed. He heard voices in the sitting-room. He strode over and flung open the door.

There knelt his wife, arms outstretched, and there were two men, one busily taking photos, the other making notes.

'What the blazes . . .?'

'Hold it there, sweetheart! That's lovely, Now – the look! Give me the look again!'

Aunt Celia was re-enacting the events of the previous night, and being photographed doing so.

'Celia!'

She turned and her arms dropped.

'What the hell do you think you're doing?'

'Ah, Mr Parker, I presume. Bill Martin, *Daily Sport*.'

'Ken Porter,' said the photographer briefly. 'D'you mind, sir, we're nearly through.'

'You're through now,' said Uncle Parker grimly. 'Come, dearest.'

He pulled his wife to her feet.

'But Russell, these gentlemen have come to record – '

'They're not gentlemen,' he told her, 'and they're not recording anything. You two – out!'

The newsmen, who had seen Uncle Parker both the previous night and that morning at the police station, had been convinced that he was in some way connected with the Knaresborough Knifer. It had not been difficult to find out from the police who he was. They had hared over to The Knoll in the hopes of an Exclusive. The story they now had was a far cry from the Knifer, but it was an Exclusive, all right.

'I gather you were here at the time, sir,' said Bill. 'Did you see this angel?'

'No I did not,' returned Uncle Parker. 'Leave angels out of it. You're trespassing.'

'And what's all this about an ancient sacred ritual?' asked

95

Ken. 'All that stuff about a goat? What goat? Any chance of a shot of that?'

'Twice blessed!' cried Aunt Celia rapturously, and looked so beautiful and ethereal that Ken raised his camera and took another shot.

'If you don't clear out now I shall send for the police.' Uncle Parker sounded more confident than he felt. He had a suspicion that any such call he made would be given very low priority.

'Come on, Mr Parker,' said Bill. 'You don't get angels calling every day. You'd be surprised how many of our readers believe in angels.'

'I would be surprised', returned Uncle Parker, 'how many of your readers can actually read. My wife is in a delicate condition, and – '

'We gathered that. Twins. Congratulations.'

This was terrible. Uncle Parker had been hoping not to have to inform his relatives that there were now twins in the offing. Now the whole world would know. Also, certain members of the family already maintained that Aunt Celia was more or less permanently out of her tree. Most of this criticism Uncle Parker smoothly deflected by explaining about her uniquely sensitive nature. He managed to make it into a plus. Now, the ancient sacred ritual of the goat and the glass was about to hit the headlines, along with a Green-Eyed Angel. This would not, he knew, look good in cold print.

He thought fast. With a daughter like Daisy and a wife like Aunt Celia, he was well used to thinking on his feet. He could have given lessons to most politicians.

'Gentlemen. Just a minute.' He jerked his head towards the door and moved towards it. The pair exchanged glances and followed him.

Once in the hall, and the sitting-room door shut, Uncle Parker lowered his voice to a conspiratorial whisper.

'She had you there, I'm afraid. Don't worry – you're not the first.'

'You what?'

'Publicity-mad,' said Uncle Parker sadly. 'Can't do anything with her. I've only to turn my back and she's on to the press with some cock and bull story or other.'

'She didn't ring *us*,' said Ken suspiciously. 'And said she'd never heard of the *Sport*.'

'She would,' Uncle Parker told him. 'All part of the act. Surely you saw that spread of her in the *News of the World* last month?

'*Why*'s she publicity-mad?' asked Bill.

Uncle Parker shrugged.

'Who knows? All part of the bid for Ophelia, I suppose.'

'The *what*?'

'Lifelong ambition,' Uncle Parker explained. 'Thinks she *is* Ophelia, half the time. Got this burning urge to play it opposite Kenneth Branagh.'

'She an actress, then?'

'Oh no. That's why she needs the publicity. Make some kind of name for herself.'

'So all that stuff about the angel . . .?'

'Angel?' said Uncle Parker. 'I ask you! What do you think?'

'Still, it is a story . . .'

'And she's a looker,' Ken added. 'Very tasty.'

Uncle Parker gave him a cold look.

'If you're after a real story,' he said, 'you want a couple of miles up the road.'

'Oh yeah? More angels?'

'Wife gone missing,' Uncle Parker told them. 'Bagthorpe's the name. Unicorn House. 'You'd better look sharp – there's some of your lot already on to it.'

Again the pair exchanged glances. Uncle Parker pressed home his point.

'Big story. She's Stella Bright.'

'What – the Agony Aunt?'

'The very same,' nodded Uncle Parker. 'Lovely woman. I could tell you a way round the back.'

They finally swallowed the bait. Uncle Parker gave them directions to the field they could cross to make their way into the Bagthorpes' garden. He felt rather mean about this, because he was, by and large, very fond of his wife's family. But he was fonder still of his wife herself, and would certainly, if push came to shove, have laid down his life for her. He saw the press men out and returned to her for an update on the Green-Eyed Angel.

Meanwhile, many miles away, another member of the Bag-thorpe ménage was having her own problems with the press.

'London?' Mrs Fosdyke cried. 'You never told me it would be in London! You said a safe 'ouse, and it *ain't* safe in London!'

'You are in the capital of the world, Mrs Fosdyke,' Ms Page told her. 'Where you belong. The Queen lives here, remember,' she added cunningly.

'Oh yes – in a great big palace with soldiers marching up and down in front! *She* knows it ain't safe.'

Mrs Fosdyke was genuinely terrified to find that she had been transported to London, which to her was a cross between Sodom and Gomorrah and war-torn Beirut. There, she understood, rapes, muggings, bombings and murders happened hourly. She had even refused to join the WI coach-party trip to go shopping and see *The Phantom of the Opera*.

'The shops in Aysham's good enough for me,' she had said. 'And they ain't full of bombs like 'Arrods. And it'll be dark when you come out that theatre, and Lord knows oo'll be about.'

Ms Page tried in vain to allay her fears. It was her own

newspaper, in part, which had helped Mrs Fosdyke build up her mental picture of the capital.

'Why not unpack your things and start to feel at home?' She suggested. 'Have you seen your bathroom?'

Mrs Fosdyke had. It had contained one of those nasty foreign bidets, and was large enough to throw a party in. In fact the whole proportions of her promised safe house were so daunting as to make her feel very much *not* at home. She had pictured something cosy – a cottage with its own little garden and a dovecote, perhaps. What she now found herself in could well have been the Iranian Embassy. She gazed nervously about her at the moulded ceilings and swagged brocade curtains, and wished herself back in her own crowded little living-room.

'I doubt I can settle 'ere,' she said.

She did indeed present a forlorn and incongruous little figure, standing there in her polyester two-piece and clutching her fur-lined boots on that vast acreage of carpet, among the gilded furniture and mirrors. Ms Page actually felt a twinge of remorse. Even she could see that Mrs Fosdyke was a fish out of water.

'You'll soon get used to it,' she urged. 'I know – why don't you put the telly on?'

Mrs Fosdyke seemed frozen there, so Ms Page did it for her. At once there came a familiar sight and sound.

'*Neighbours*!' she said, and sat down suddenly. She sat and watched the episode in silence. She was indeed reassured by the presence of these familiar characters, part of her extended family.

'Well!' she said when it was over. 'I should 'ave put 'er down as 'aving more sense than that! There'll be trouble there, you mark my words!'

She shook her head over the folly of the blonde Australian matron who was one of her favourite characters.

'I'm 'ungry,' she announced.

'Me too!' agreed Ms Page.

Mrs Fosdyke had declined to grab a bite at one of the

motorway service areas, and had given her opinion of such places in no uncertain terms. These were just the kind of views Ms Page's editor was after, and she had made copious notes. She had some excellent stuff about how poison from cling film leaks into sandwiches, and about chips being coated with poisonous brown colouring to make them look more enticing.

It now occurred to the reporter that it would be fun to take Mrs Fosdyke to an exclusive West End restaurant, and get her reactions to that. It would make a nice contrast.

'Shouldn't think the old bat's ever heard of Boeuf Bourguignon, let alone eaten it,' she thought.

That, of course, is where she was wrong. Working for the *Sludge* newspaper as she did, Patsy Page naturally thought in stereotypes. Having seen Mrs Fosdyke in her home surroundings, she had assumed that she boiled greens for half an hour and poured tomato ketchup over everything. Whereas, had Mrs Fosdyke had the right clothes and accent, she could easily have become an Inspector for the *Good Food Guide*. In fact, she could have set up her own bistro and featured *in* it. As it was, her talents lay unsung and undiscovered, wasted on the desert air of Unicorn House.

At first Mrs Fosdyke was dubious about the wisdom of venturing out, but was assured that the car would take them from door to door.

'It ain't one of them 'amburger and chicken places, is it?' she asked suspiciously.

Ms Page laughingly assured her that it was not. It was the kind of place where cabinet ministers ate, she said, and television stars.

'What – like Bob Monkhouse and Esther Rantzen?'

Certainly, Ms Page said. Such stars could easily be seated at the very next table. (Her editor paid good money to ensure that his reporters were given tables within eavesdropping distance of their quarries.)

Once at the restaurant Mrs Fosdyke devoted her attention to her fellow-diners rather than the menu. She did this quite openly, swivelling about in her seat and straining forward to peer past pillars. Her efforts were eventually rewarded. She sighted a well-known magician, and kept a vigilant eye on him in the hopes, perhaps, of seeing a dove flutter from his sleeve, or a billiard ball emerge from his ear.

''E's ever so good,' she told her companion. 'An' I daresay 'e can bend knives and forks, if 'e wants to.'

'Speaking of which,' said Ms Page, 'shall we order?'

She passed the menu over to Mrs Fosdyke and awaited her reaction. She was hoping for some succintly expressed disapproval that she could headline FOZZY FAILS FANCY FROG FARE.

Mrs Fosdyke appeared to be studying the menu with intense concentration. Given that it was in French, Ms Page assumed that her guest was having difficulty with the translation.

'What about the Boeuf Bourguignon?' she suggested. 'That's topside of beef, with bacon, simmered in a sauce of – '

'I know what it is!' snapped Mrs Fosdyke. 'And I ain't come all the way to London to eat things I can do at 'ome any day of the week. I'll 'ave the snails, and the mutton with capers.'

This fairly stumped Ms Page, who in her time had wined and dined many a celebrity who had thought that *escargots* was probably French for 'asparagus', and had a very nasty shock when they arrived complete with shells.

'On the other 'and,' mused Mrs Fosdyke, 'I'm very partial to vichyssoise and them oysters sound nice. I don't know . . . oh, go on – I'll have the snails. Mrs Bagthorpe don't go in for them. She's a bit what you might call 'idebound when it comes to food.'

On and on she prattled. She was enchanted by the menu, and by the food when it arrived.

'At least them French know 'ow to cook,' she observed, thus at a stroke kyboshing the proposed headline.

'Ah, but they have their faults, don't they?' prompted Patsy Page.

'Do they?' Mrs Fosdyke was savouring her dish. 'I should say there's a touch more garlic than in mine – they say they are a bit 'eavy-'anded with the garlic.'

'But in other matters,' her hostess leaned forward. 'You know – *vive la différence!*'

'The what? The only French I know's for cooking. Viv what?'

'You know – sex!'

Mrs Fosdyke put down her fork.

'That's a funny sort of word to come out with when people is eating,' she said accusingly. 'It's disgusting.'

'You mean – the French are?'

'I don't 'old with it. There's far too much of it, in my opinion.'

This was better. Ms Page thought it insensitive to whip out her notepad, but made mental notes as best she could. It appeared that Mrs Fosdyke had no time at all for sex. People had done without it for hundreds and hundreds of years, and now all of a sudden it was all over everywhere. It was all over the papers (it certainly was in the tabloids she favoured) and everlastingly all over the telly – it was even creeping into *Neighbours*. It took all of the romance out of everything. If there was one thing she couldn't stand it was the sight of people with their clothes off.

'Like skinned rabbits,' she said. ''Orrible. You wonder what they see in each other. You won't catch *me* with my clothes off!'

She looked challengingly at Ms Page, as if daring her to request a photo opportunity.

'Oh, clothes make all the difference,' she agreed weakly.

'And speaking of which – what about a shopping spree?'

She had plenty of 'before' photographs of Mrs Fosdyke. What she was now after were some 'after' shots.

'And how about a facial and a manicure?'

Mrs Fosdyke looked down at her work-worn hands and unpolished nails.

'Ooh, I ain't never 'ad one of them! Oooh, wait till I tell Flo and Mavis! Can we get some postcards? Always send' em a card, I do – 'cept that time I went to Wales. Did I tell you about Wales? Ooh, you'd never believe . . .'

She was off. Sex was forgotten. Mrs Fosdyke was back on familiar and well-worn tracks.

Meanwhile, back at Unicorn House, there were further problems with the press. The reporter and photographer had followed Uncle Parker's directions, and set off across the meadow to effect a back-way entry into the Bagthorpes' garden.

'Stella Bright, eh?' said Ken. 'The wife once wrote to her.'

'Oh yeah? About you, was it? Husband out all hours and drinking like a fish?'

'You can cut that out,' Ken told him. 'Your wife left you. It was about the kids, as a matter of fact. Playing her up. Stopping out all hours.'

'And what'd she say?'

'A lot of stuff about Deep Breathing and Positive Thinking.'

'You what?'

'Calmed the wife down a treat, but the kids went from bad to worse.'

'Gone missing . . . could be her own problems got on top of her and she's cleared off.'

'Or one of her clients topped her.'

Either way, it was a good story. The pair found the stile and climbed over it. Cautiously they made their way through the long grass and shrubbery.

'Better go steady,' Ken warned. 'These country types tend to keep Rottweilers.'

They eventually emerged by the Dead Sea. They stared in

disbelief at the horrible swirl of weed and curdled milk. Here and there floated the livid, swollen belly of a dead fish.

'What the hell's been going on?'

'Look!' Bill pointed.

There on the brink lay Daisy's abandoned saucepan and the two fish on a plate. It looked like a Salvador Dali still life.

'Get a shot of it, Ken!'

Photographing the fish at least cut them down to size, made the whole scenario more manageable, less surreal. The pair continued on their way with added caution.

'Listen!'

They stopped.

'Oo a bad boy! How oo get out, you an't got no fingers!' (Even had Billy Goat Gruff been unusual in having fingers instead of hoofs, he would still have been in the shed. It had no handle on the inside.)

'A kid!' whispered Ken.

They tiptoed forward and parting the bushes saw Daisy Parker and her goat. To their untutored eyes, Daisy looked harmless enough, with her frilly frock and golden ringlets, but neither man had ever seen a goat got up like this before. It was positively festooned with bells and ribbons.

'I's going to mack you,' Daisy informed him. 'Mack mack mack!'

She dealt three blows that were clearly water off a duck's back to the goat, which in fact nuzzled her affectionately. She pushed him away.

'I got annunner prison for you,' she told him. 'An' it got even *more* spiders.'

Then, with her amazingly sharp eyes, she saw the newspapermen. Her eyes widened.

'Oo you?' she demanded.

The pair emerged somewhat sheepishly from the greenery.

'Hello, little girl,' said Bill. 'What's your name?'

'What oo doing in der and what's *your* name?' she countered.

'I'm Bill and he's Ken.'

'Do you know my Grandma Bag?'

'Er – well, no.'

'Cos you mustn't let her out of prison. She dot to stop der and be sorry.'

'Well, yes, that is the general idea,' agreed Bill, thinking to humour her.

A thought struck Daisy.

'Is oo strangers?' she asked.

'Strangers?' echoed Ken unsuspectingly. 'Well, yes, you could say that.'

'An' have oo got sweeties?'

Ken had, as a matter of fact, recently made one of his half-hearted attempts to give up smoking, and carried a bag of boiled sweets as a substitute.

'Sure.' He fished in his pocket for the bag and proffered it. 'Here – have one.'

Daisy backed away, eyeing the bag with profound suspicion. Memories were surfacing of Grandma's warnings about sweets and strangers. Up till now, Daisy had been uncertain exactly what a stranger looked like, but now thought she knew. If these were strangers, then they should be in prison. The only trouble was that she was running out of prisons. Grandma was in the potting-shed, from which Billy Goat Gruff had inexplicably escaped. Daisy had earmarked for him an outhouse where the Bagthorpes kept their deck-chairs and a spare deep-freeze. Where, then, would she put the strangers?

In the manner of many a judge before her she made a snap decision. Billy Goat Gruff was reprieved.

'I changed my mind,' she told the goat. 'Oo'll have to go to prison annunner day.'

She then turned to the pressmen and gave them a beam of outstanding radiance and guilelessness. The two men, with not a misgiving in the world, smiled back.

'Er – you wouldn't know where Mrs Bagthorpe is, lovey?' asked Bill.

'Oh yes,' replied Daisy untruthfully.

'If we could just have a word . . .?'

'Oo come wiv me,' she told them. 'I show you.'

She gave Billy Goat Gruff's rein a sharp tug and set off towards the house. The two men followed her. They were hardened types, both of them. They had seen action in the inner cities, and attended sieges. They saw their current investigations as a little light relief. By now, they should have learned that appearances can be deceptive. They had seen the arrest of clergymen, and of murderers who looked as if butter would not melt in their mouths. Admittedly they had never before encountered a four-year-old delinquent with golden curls. But some sure instinct should have told them to watch their backs, that this was Attila the Hun in sheep's clothing.

What happened to them next, then, was probably a salutary lesson. It was karma.

As they approached the rear of the house Daisy took a good look round.

'Der's nobody der,' she informed the pressmen. 'But you better watch out cos Uncle Bag's a bad bad man. He been in prison.'

She really did have prison on the brain. She led the pair to the outhouse, and saw with delight that there was a key to turn and throw away.

'Auntie Bag in there,' she informed them.

They were startled by this intelligence. The place appeared to be windowless. Daisy stood on tiptoe and turned the key. The men braced themselves for what could be the unpleasant sight of a defunct Stella Bright. The door swung open. The man peered past Daisy into the dim interior. It seemed to contain only a few deck-chairs and a large chest deep-freeze.

106

'She in der.' Daisy pointed to the latter.

At this point they should have probably burst into the house, found the telephone and called the police. But neither man had so far ever actually discovered a murder victim. This was News with a capital N. Ken could actually photograph the body – something the police would never allow in a million years. Stella Bright – in a deep-freeze! All these thoughts ran through their heads.

'Go on,' Daisy urged. 'Look!' She needed them in there before she could slam the door on them, lock it and throw away the key.

It was an invitation they could not refuse. They both went in.

'Der!' cried the triumphant Daisy. 'Got you!'

She slammed the door. She turned the key, pulled it out and threw it away. God was in his heaven and all was right with the world. From within came the clatter of falling deck-chairs and a string of muffled curses.

'You jus' stop der and be sorry!' she called.

The door trembled under a mighty kick. It would not give way. The house had been built when they knew how to build houses.

'An' jus be quiet!' she told them. 'If oo don't be quiet, oo'll stop der for ever and ever!'

Their reply was inaudible. Daisy turned and beamed at the docile Billy Goat Gruff. Now her career as gaoler had really taken off. She felt that she could lock up the whole world.

Nine

Mrs Bagthorpe allowed Tess to take a taxi into Aysham with her list. She still had not broken the news to her family that Max was to be a guest, and had warned Jack not to do so. At present they were hungry and bad-tempered.

'Bring us back some of that lovely Italian takeaway,' she told Tess. 'It will be a lovely change, and I'm sure we shall manage splendidly without dear Mrs Fosdyke.'

Tess did a very thorough shop (narrowly missing running into her father several times) and returned with at least a hundred pounds' worth of goodies. The rest did, indeed, cheer up at the sight of these, and willingly helped put them all away in the fridge, larder and deep-freeze. (Unfortunately for the pressmen the spare freezer was not brought into play.) While they did so the Italian takeaways were placed in the oven to reheat and fill the kitchen with pleasing aromas. Rosie laid the table.

'Where's Grandma?' she asked.

No one knew.

'And Daisy,' Jack added. 'Where's Daisy?'

He remembered her angling activities down by the pool, and wondered if he should check. Mrs Bagthorpe went up in search of Grandma, but returned with only Grandpa, who had been watching television with the sound turned down.

'She is not there,' she told the others. 'Though she seems to be progressing well with her memoirs. I'm *so* pleased about that.'

She had not, naturally, paused to read the memoirs, or she might have been less pleased. She did not herself think Mr Bagthorpe perfect, but did like to think of him as at least human.

'I see you have brought plenty, Tess,' she said approvingly, as the food was brought out of the oven. She had indeed. With true Bagthorpian overkill she had informed the Italians that lunch for at least a dozen was required. 'We will leave some in the oven for seconds, and for the others when they come.'

She knew that there was now an extra mouth to feed, and her brow clouded slightly as she remembered her promise to Max. Everyone sat down and started forking up spaghetti and meatballs or lasagne, and mellowing in the process. Mrs Bagthorpe judged that her moment had come.

'I have a lovely surprise for you all,' she began.

'What, Mother?' inquired William through a mouthful of lasagne. 'Goat face down in the Dead Sea, is it?'

The rest, with the exception of Jack, tittered.

'I have brought a visitor back with me.'

'A visitor? Where from?'

'From Mrs Fosdyke's house, where I stayed overnight.'

None of her progeny apart from Jack had shown any interest in where she had been.

'So where is this visitor?'

Mrs Bagthorpe hesitated.

'In the garden.'

'Oh, I see. Some lunatic botanist. World expert on lobelias.'

'As a matter of fact . . .' she concentrated hard on her Breathing. 'It is Mrs Fosdyke's son, Max.'

'*What?*'

'Max,' she repeated firmly. 'Surely you remember him?'

'I thought he'd run off,' said Rosie. 'Ages ago. *I* don't remember him.'

'Lucky you,' Tess told her. 'Why've you brought him here? To *visit*?'

'He has returned home like the Prodigal Son,' said Mrs Bagthorpe, with a fine disregard for accuracy. Mrs Fosdyke had come nearer to killing Max than any fatted calf.

She pressed gamely on.

'Unfortunately, he is in trouble with the police.'

'Oh yes?' said William. 'And we're going to harbour him? That makes us accessories after the crime. You should know that.'

'It is only a minor matter involving a cash card,' said Mrs Bagthorpe, who usually took such matters very seriously indeed. 'And he will eventually go to the police.'

'After he's pinched everyone else's cash cards,' William said. 'You can't be serious.'

'I am going to save him!' she cried, and they all looked up, startled. She was alight with missionary zeal. 'Rehabiliate him into society. He has been sleeping rough.'

William groaned.

'Not another! How long since *he* had a bath? And talking of which – what's happened to that stinking tramp?'

'He went to The Knoll with Uncle Park,' Jack said.

'I should dearly like a stuffed egg,' said Grandpa wistfully.

They all looked at him. He rarely made any contribution to the brisk and civilized exchange of views and opinions that was meant to characterize Bagthorpian mealtimes. He lived in a world of Selective Deafness and television images, and spent long hours by the water's edge fishing, and seemed a genuinely happy man.

'I'll make you some stuffed eggs, Grandpa,' Rosie told him.

'And me,' said Tess jealously. 'It's my turn tonight.'

'I should think any fool could do stuffed eggs,' William said. 'Even Jack.'

'There's no one who can stuff an egg like dear Mrs Fosdyke,' Grandpa went on. 'Where *is* Mrs Fosdyke?'

He had probably not missed her till now because she did not

impinge much on his life. He could not hear the unholy rattling she set up at the sink, or her frenetic hoovering.

'She has gone on a little holiday, dear,' said Mrs Bagthorpe swiftly.

'To a safe house,' Jack added.

The others hooted.

'Fozzy – at a safe house! Gone to live with Salman Rushdie!'

'*Why*, for heaven's sake?'

They would soon discover.

Now that Grandpa had surfaced he seemed unstoppable.

'Where is Henry?' he asked. 'Where is Mr O'Toole? Where are Grace and Daisy?'

This was a long list of missing persons. One or two present did have misgivings at the realization that Grandma and Daisy had gone missing together. They were known in the family as the Unholy Alliance, not without cause. On this occasion, however, Grandma was building up an Alliance of a very different sort . . .

It was a severe shock to Grandma to find herself so heartlessly cast into prison by her favourite. She had never really plumbed Daisy's depths as most of the rest of the family had. When she called her 'a shining jewel of a child' she genuinely believed this. Besides, Grandma liked action, and when Daisy was around there usually was action – often involving the police. Grandma adored any kind of dealings with the constabulary, and was probably addicted. Also, Daisy drove Mr Bagthorpe to the limits of his endurance, and this was bound to be a plus in Grandma's book.

'I expect it is just a little joke,' she told herself, and for some moments waited expectantly by the door. When it did not open, and there was no response to her repeated calling, she moved over to the window just in time to see the shining jewel skipping off into the shrubbery.

Grandma's abrupt incarceration came as a very nasty shock to Max, too. He cowered trembling under his sacks, praying to be made invisible. He knew who his fellow-prisoner was, all right. She had scared the living daylights out of him as a child. He had huddled in broom cupboards and dodged behind sofas to escape her basilisk eye. He now wished he had given himself up to the police. He wished he was safely in a proper prison.

Grandma was not one to sit around twiddling her thumbs. Once she realized that she was due to spend some time in the shed, she began to take stock of it. Almost immediately she spotted the suspect pile of sacks, with a pair of dirty trainers protruding from them at one end, and a mat of hair at the other.

Grandma was a game old bird, but did not like the look of this. She had been avidly following the progress of the Knaresborough Knifer. This, she realized, could be he. While her dearest ambition was to become a witness of a serious crime, it was no part of her plans to become the *victim* of one.

She had already discovered that the door had no handle on the inside. If she smashed the window there was no way she could clamber up and go through it fast enough to escape.

'I shall have to talk him out of it,' she thought. She was aware that this was an option. Granted, it was one usually employed in the case of hostage-takers, but there was a principle involved. If you built up a rapport with someone who had you in his power, he was less likely to do you harm. She thereupon determined to build up such a rapport.

She was not sure how to set about this. At present the criminal believed himself to be concealed. (Had she only known it, he was desperately uninterested in building up any kind of rapport, and the pair could have spent their entire incarceration in total silence, had Grandma let well alone.)

First, Grandma coughed – not an ordinary cough, but the kind you manufacture as a primitive opening gambit. She coughed again. There was no response from the heap of sacking.

'I would not hurt a fly,' she went on. 'I am a lover of all creatures great and small, even the lowest forms of human life, even murderers. I love them all.'

If she hoped that whoever was under the sacks would recognize himself from this description, and fling back his coverings exclaiming 'Love me!', she was disappointed. Max, still trembling, was thinking that people who talk to themselves are generally held to be mad.

Grandma dimly felt that if there was to be any encounter between herself and the Knifer it would be best for herself to make the first move. Any first move on his part might take the form of his suddenly leaping up, knife in hand. This would not allow for any kind of dialogue. She drew a deep breath.

'Excuse me . . . '

A sudden twitch of the sacking.

'Excuse me, is there someone there? I do hope so.'

A low groan emitted from the sacks. Slowly a form straightened itself and emerged, and a face appeared. It wore a look of wild desperation that could easily be misinterpreted as blood-lust. Grandma quaked but held her ground.

'Oh, there is!' she cried with extreme gaiety. 'Oh, how lovely! I am Mrs Grace Bagthorpe – how do you do?'

She actually stretched out a hand. Max, clutching his sacks about him for comfort, stared at it.

'I don't believe we have met,' she said in her best social manner.

Grandma was looking into a face she had seen many times before, albeit years previously. She had never, however, seen it properly. She had a kind of tunnel vision that saw only what it wished to see, and ignored the unwelcome or uninteresting. As a child, Max had been both these things. (Also, of course, he had spent much of his time dodging her.)

'I'm Max,' he muttered.

'Oh – Max – of course – Max!' Grandma frantically and vainly racked her brains. 'Whatever are you doing here, Max?'

' 'Iding,' he responded.

'What an excellent place you have picked!' she told him. 'Hardly anyone comes in here but my daughter-in-law, and she is almost blind.' (Mrs Bagthorpe had recently taken to wearing spectacles for reading.) 'And as far as I am concerned, my lips are sealed. Oh yes, I shall not breathe a word, I swear it!'

She looked hopefully about her but there was, naturally enough, no Bible to swear on.

'Fanks,' Max said.

The old bat was not as bad as he had remembered. Mad, but not so bad. She was certainly preferable to the goat that had run out at him.

'I ain't stopping,' he told her. 'No fear!'

'It is certainly not very comfortable,' Grandma agreed. 'I would not be here myself by choice.'

' 'Ere,' said Max, climbing to his feet. 'Sit on 'ere.'

He placed one of the empty sacks on a crate and indicated the makeshift seat.

'What a perfect gentleman!' cried Grandma, and took it. She felt rather as she imagined Queen Elizabeth I must have done, when Sir Walter Raleigh spread out his cloak for her. Her efforts at building up a rapport were bearing early fruit.

'Now, Max, tell me all about yourself.'

He squatted at her feet. It was years since anyone had shown the least interest in him.

'Not much to tell,' he said.

He did, nevertheless, tell her, starting with his running off from home.

'No one could've lived there! And it's still the same – seen it last night – 'ad to sleep there!' He shuddered.

'How dreadful,' murmured Grandma, imagining some rat-infested hovel.

114

'Ma never listened,' he went on. 'And she was always off at your place, and cooking *you* things.'

'Ah!' At last the penny dropped. Max Fosdyke, the runaway son! He could still, of course, be the Knaresborough Knifer, but Grandma doubted this. She could not see Mrs Fosdyke as the mother of a serial killer.

'You must have felt terribly neglected,' she told him, keeping up the rapport.

It worked like a charm. Max told her everything, over all the missing years, and ending with the landlady in Bridlington.

'So the pigs is after me,' he ended glumly.

Grandma was enchanted – the Police Factor! In normal circumstances she would have played for time till her release, then gone straight to the phone and rung the police or *Crimewatch UK*. But the theory of rapport had rebounded on her. It evidently worked both ways. She found herself on the side of the criminal. The intimacy built up between them in that dusty potting-shed had formed an indissoluble bond. She was, she realized, now an accessory after the fact. She cared not a fig. (She had always been fascinated by the police, but never frightened of them.)

'What a wonderfully interesting and colourful life you have had,' she told Max. 'You should write your memoirs.'

Max, in his turn, was flattered.

'D'you reckon?'

'Certainly I do,' she told him. 'I am writing my own, but my life has been very uneventful, I fear.' This was a curious way of describing life as lived by the Bagthorpes.

'Mrs Bagthorpe junior reckons I should give meself up,' he said.

'What nonsense!' she cried. 'Why should you do their detecting for them? Let them do their own detecting!'

'She says if I clean up and cut me 'air they could let me off.'

'Pay no attention to her,' Grandma said. 'She is unhinged. If

115

you wish, Max, I will take you under my own wing.'

This, against all the odds, struck him as an attractive proposition. From what he remembered, Grandma usually got her own way. If she had decided that he did not deserve to go to prison, then he would not go.

'OK. Fanks.' Now it was his turn to stretch out a hand. Grandma took and shook it, delighted. Shaking hands with a wanted criminal beat swearing on the Bible hands down.

Another Unholy Alliance had been formed.

When the receptionist of the Crown and Mitre watched Mr Bagthorpe go to his car she was not quite sure what she was expecting, but it was certainly not what she actually saw.

'A Hoover!'

This seemed an unlikely weapon for a building society robbery. On the other hand, it did seem sinister. To date, no visitor to the hotel had brought a Hoover as part of his luggage. Nor did people tend to take such an item on holiday. As she watched, Mr Bagthorpe slammed shut his boot and set off back across the yard, dragging the contraption behind him on the cobbles with a horrible clatter.

This reassured the receptionist. Surely, no criminal would advertise his activities in such a way? She decided that he must be the kind of neurotic who is terrified of germs, and had brought the Hoover to use in his room. Such people did exist. They would ring down to reception gibbering about hairs found in the bath, or to demand a change of room because they had detected a crack in the lavatory bowl.

It was in order to reassure such clients that the chambermaids at the Crown and Mitre were instructed to pleat the end of the toilet roll into a neat triangle, and place a sealed strip across the lavatory seat. (These practices infuriated Mr Bagthorpe almost as much as the soaps and bath essences. He said that one reason for the astronomical prices charged by hotels was the time wasted practising origami on toilet rolls. His children would sometimes while away a moment in similar fashion, hoping to be rewarded by enraged bellows during a later visit by their father.)

Whatever Mr Bagthorpe's faults, he could not be accused of over-fastidiousness on the hygiene front – rather the reverse. He very rarely allowed Mrs Fosdyke into his study to clean, and maintained that most of the vacuuming done was with intent to wear out his carpets, and drive himself into writer's block. He frequently quoted Quentin Crisp's dictum that, if left, dust reached its own natural level, and never got worse after two years.

The receptionist ran back to her station and hurriedly informed the manager of the development. They waited in vain for some time for Mr Bagthorpe to reappear in the lobby with his Hoover. Had his address on the booking form been legible, they might have come to the correct conclusion that he was taking it in for service. On the other hand, they would then have wondered why one who lived only a mile or so away should book into the hotel in the first place.

'At least we know his car number now,' the manager said. 'Write it down, Dilys.'

Mr Bagthorpe dumped the Hoover at the repair shop with relief, and set about providing himself with toiletries. He bought a tube of toothpaste and a purple toothbrush, then a cheap tablet of soap, so that he would not have to give the Crown and Mitre the satisfaction of using theirs. He took these items back to his room, little knowing that the time of his return was being logged by the alert receptionist.

He sat for a while attempting the *Guardian* crossword but soon became restless. He usually took a bottle of Scotch with him on visits to hotels, and realized that he was without this crutch. He accordingly set off to purchase it.

The receptionist noted the time of his going out and that of his return, shortly afterwards, carrying a bag bearing the name

117

of a well-known chain of liquor stores. She was made nervous by this development. She knew of the role often played by drink in violent crime. She also imagined that holding up a building society must be quite frightening, and that people who did so would probably require some Dutch courage before embarking on such an enterprise. She contacted the manager again.

He was well aware that some guests brought their own drink with them to avoid paying exorbitant prices at the bar, and he deplored this practice. But that Mr Bagthorpe should have his own supply of Scotch in his wardrobe was, he admitted, a shade worrying.

'But we mustn't overreact, Dilys,' he said. 'There is no law against it.'

'But there must be a law against what he's going to do when he's drunk it!' she protested. 'And by then it'll be too late. The police are always asking the public to be on the alert and report things. It's part of crime prevention.'

The manager's own view of the police at present coincided more or less with that of Mr Bagthorpe. His house had been burgled some weeks previously, and when they arrived the police had not even bothered to dust for fingerprints. They had said it was a waste of time. They said that these days burglaries were so commonplace that if they spent their time dusting for fingerprints they would be doing nothing else from dawn till dusk. When they left they had advised him to keep an eye on local car-boot sales.

'Half the stuff nicked ends up there,' they had said.

Since then, the manager and his wife had spent every weekend touring car-boot sales. They had picked up one or two items at knock-down prices, but had so far failed to spot the solid brass carriage clock given to his wife's father on retirement, or his own brand-new camcorder. It occurred to him that this latter would have been useful now, to record the suspect guest's activities.

118

Mr Bagthorpe had by no means finished once he had stowed the Scotch in his wardrobe. He frequently proclaimed that it was not in his nature to sit around idling, and this was true. He was as fidgety as a tick.

He toyed with the idea of ringing Uncle Parker, and having another go at him about payment for the pool. He then remembered that hotels often make inflated charges for phone calls, so shelved the idea. As a writer, he could have played around with some ideas, made a few notes.

'I can't work in this hell-hole,' he told himself. 'The vibes are all to pot.'

Mr Bagthorpe was by no means New Age or mystical in his thinking, but he did go on a lot about vibrations, and claimed that he could not write a single word unless these were right. He had even installed an ionizer in his study, to 'suck up' any hostile vibrations set up by Mrs Fosdyke while she was in there cleaning. For him, people had vibrations as well as places, and he said that Daisy's were such that it was a wonder that the grass did not blacken under her feet, and foliage shrivel and die in her path. His own mother's magnetic field he put more or less on a par with that of Medusa.

Given that the Crown and Mitre had the wrong vibrations, and that he had given up on the crossword, Mr Bagthorpe moodily cast around for some alternative activity. It suddenly struck him that he had no electric razor with him, and would be stumped in the morning. He had no intention of forking out for a new one. He toyed with the idea of starting a beard. The trouble was that he was usually scathing about the people who wore them.

'Wonder what *he's* hiding under there,' he would say, when Brian Redhead or Terry Waite appeared on the TV screen. 'He should be held down and forcibly shaved, and let us all see.'

He never specified what these hidden things might be, but implied darkly that they were something a lot worse than a weak chin.

119

'I'll go out and get one of those cut-throats,' he decided.

Back past the receptionist's desk he went. Another time was duly logged. Back he came. Another entry. Back in his room, Mr Bagthorpe remembered that shaving soap, which he had not used since adolescence, would be needed. Back to the High Street he sallied.

The receptionist now began to favour the theory that he might be a bomber, rather than a bank robber. She knew that there had been a bomb incident in nearby Passingham the previous day, and that the man involved had not yet been caught. She thought that Mr Bagthorpe probably kept nipping out to buy ingredients for making a bomb. She herself did not know how to make a bomb, and the method had certainly never been shown on *Blue Peter*, but she gathered that the ingredients were quite common-place, and the assembly of them as simple as making a pencil case from a squeezee washing-up liquid container.

She confided this theory to the manager. He had been reluctant to aid the police by reporting a bank robber, but a bomber was a very different kettle of fish. If his hotel were blown up, he would be out of a job. On the other hand, he would look extremely silly if Mr Bagthorpe turned out to be harmless, and the incident would be bound to be reported. People might not want to stay at the Crown and Mitre. They might even not wish to drink there. Either way, his career would be on the line.

'Let us not overreact, Dilys,' he told her. 'You need Semtex to make bombs, you know.'

'But you can get that at W H Smith!' shrieked the reception-ist, confusing it with Tipp-Ex.

The manager smiled indulgently, patted her and told her not to worry her pretty little head. (It was lucky for him that she was not boned up on sexual stereotyping.)

As they stood there the lift doors opened and Mr Bagthorpe emerged. He made for the revolving doors.

The manager's brow furrowed . . .

120

Ten

When the men from the *Daily Drivel*, whose cars Uncle Parker had spotted near the drive to Unicorn House, knocked on the door, it was William who answered. They flashed their press cards and asked for Mr Bagthorpe.

'He's not here,' William told them. 'And even if he were he wouldn't talk to you.'

This was probably not true. Mr Bagthorpe might have talked, but what he said would have been unprintable.

'But he was released last night,' said One. 'Surely he's come back home?'

'Of course he did,' replied William. 'But now he's cleared off again, as per usual.'

The newsmen were mystified by this. Given that Mrs Bagthorpe was Missing, they had assumed that the remaining parent would be looking after his children – at least until his arrest for the murder of his wife.

'And I don't suppose he'll be home till the cows are,' William added.

'You must be worried about your mother, sonny,' said Two.

William glared at him.

'Not at all,' he replied coldly. 'Are you worried about yours?'

'Not quite the point, sonny,' said One. 'Who was the guy at the station with your dad?'

'What? Oh, Uncle Park, I expect,' said William. 'If you're

121

after a story, who don't you go after him?'

'Er – why would we do that?' asked One.

'Well, at least he's probably at home,' William said. 'He's got a stinking tramp living with him – that'd make a story. Goes round wearing frocks and drinks Scotch like mother's milk.'

William was not to know that Mr O'Toole had been abducted by a taxi-driver.

'A cross-dressing tramp?' Two's eyes widened. This was beginning to look like a story.

'Absolutely,' said William. 'Two miles up the road – The Knoll. Can't miss it.' And shut the door.

He felt quite pleased with himself, even without the knowledge that Uncle Parker had treacherously played much the same trick on the Bagthorpes.

'Damn!' he thought as he climbed back up to his room and drums. 'Should've told 'em about Daisy.'

He could have told them about her fire-raising and slaughter of innocent goldfish. He could have shopped her for cruelty to maggots and goats.

'They're always on about abused children,' he thought. 'They could've turned it on its head: 'ABUSING CHILD DESTROYS FAMILY.'

The abusing child was at present in the kitchen looking for bread and water. She knew that this was recommended fare for prisoners, and that it was her duty, as gaoler, to supply it. Nobody else took much notice of her. Tess was deep in her recipe books, Jack was trying to remove from the cooker the grease splashed during the previous night's fry-up, and Mrs Bagthorpe was arranging a selection of Italian dishes to take out to Max.

'Dey really only s'pose to have crusses,' remarked Daisy, pulling a large brown load from the bin. She started to tear at it with her tiny fingers to remove the crust. The shreds were dropped into a silver foil dish smeared with congealed bolognese sauce.

122

'I don't think they should have no nice water out the tap,' she decided. 'Dey's too bad.'

She trotted out, making for the pond, whose water she judged more fitting for felons. Not far behind her went Mrs Bagthorpe, carrying a tray bearing a steaming plateful of Italian and a glass of nice tap water. On reaching the shed she placed the tray carefully on the ground, and straightened up to open the door. As she did so, she heard the unmistakable sound of voices from within.

It was lucky that the tray was already on the ground. Mrs Bagthorpe was quite thunder-struck.

Grandma and Max did not even hear her arrival. They were playing The Professor's Cat to while away the time. As a rule, Grandma did not join in this game – she preferred something more competitive. There was no scope for cheating in this game, and no one won. The pair had in fact achieved a few games of Noughts and Crosses by drawing in the dust with their fingers, but had run out of dust. They had also played I-spy, but as Grandma never admitted it when someone named the object she had chosen, Max had become fed up and refused to play. He challenged her to name her object, but she claimed she had forgotten.

'When you get to my age, memory plays tricks,' she said. 'I win.'

Max had never played The Professor's Cat before, and his memory was not up to much either, especially for words he had never heard before. As Mrs Bagthorpe stood riveted by the door, Grandma was reciting the list so far.

'The Professor's Cat is abstemious, black, charismatic, daft, egalitarian, fat, gargantuan, heavy, idiosyncratic, jammy . . .' she paused, pondered, then, 'kleptomaniac! she exclaimed triumphantly (and some might have thought insensitively).

'You what?' said Max, not for the first time.

Fortunately they were interrupted before Grandma could explain the meaning of the word.

'Mother!' cried Mrs Bagthorpe, and rattled the knob. She gave it a severe twist to the left and the door opened. 'Whatever are you doing here?'

'Why ever should I not be?' parried Grandma. She had no wish to shop Daisy, and in any case thought that the truth might make her look rather silly. 'You should have the door handle attended to, Laura. It does not open from the inside.'

Max's nose twitched as the smell of the Italian drifted in. He scrambled to his feet, dived past Mrs Bagthorpe, then sat and started forking it in.

'I am rather hungry myself,' Grandma remarked. 'Though I had not noticed it till now. Max and I have been having the most fascinating conversation.'

Mrs Bagthorpe was much put out to hear this. She had thought of Max as her own protégé. He was, for the moment, the centre of her universe, her *raison d'être*.

'I shall take him under my wing,' continued Grandma, correctly guessing this.

'No! He is under *my* wing!'

'You have quite sufficient on your plate, Laura,' said Grandma, mixing the metaphor.

At this point Daisy trotted up bearing her bread and water. She was furious at finding her prisoner on the loose. Max, of course, she knew nothing of.

'You *naughty* fing!' she squealed. 'What you doing out of prison?'

'It is your aunt's fault,' replied Grandma.

'Oo bad Auntie Bag!' Daisy ran at her and delivered a hard kick on the shin, thereby splashing curdled pond water over them both.

Most people would have instinctively retaliated by giving Daisy a good slap, and Mrs Bagthorpe was sorely tempted to do so. However she held very strong beliefs about the rights and dignity of the child. She had never slapped one in her life, and

124

was certainly not going to start now, with Grandma as witness. When people wrote in to Stella Bright asking whether or not they should chastise their offspring, they would receive in reply a whole spiel of stuff about the fragility of the developing ego, and the innate wisdom of the child.

No one could call Daisy's ego fragile, and her innate wisdom was questionable, but she did come under the heading of child, and as such could have kicked Mrs Bagthorpe's shins to jelly with impunity.

'Now oo's spilt Grandma's drink!' she shrieked. 'Oo dat?'

She meant Max, still busy with spaghetti.

'That is a fellow-prisoner,' Grandma told her. 'His name is Max, and you and I are going to help him.'

'Does he belong to dat Mr Toole? He got a dirty face and mixed-up hair and – '

Grandma swiftly interrupted this string of personal remarks.

'No, Daisy. As a matter of fact he belongs to Mrs Fosdyke.'

Daisy's eyes widened. Probably, like most others, she found it hard to see that lady as a mother.

'Mrs Fozzy? Where she? Has she gone to prison?'

'I don't believe so,' Grandma said. She did not tell Daisy about the safe house, because she was jealous about this.

'*I* should be taken to a safe house,' she had declared when told about it. 'This house is anything but safe.'

'Why do we not go back to the house,' suggested Mrs Bagthorpe, 'so that Max can enjoy his meal in more civilized surr – '

Her voice trailed away as she saw that the plate was almost empty. She was used to seeing people wolf their food, but Max would have won any gobbling contest hands down.

'If oo like,' said Daisy, eyeing him, 'I can put oo in prison.'

All this talk of prison was making Max nervous.

'Der's lots of people in prison,' she told him, meaning the two pressmen.

'We have already played that game, Daisy,' Grandma told her. 'We must think of something more original.'

Mrs Bagthorpe, seeing her protégé's nervousness, said swiftly, 'Let us go up to the house now, Max, and we will find you some pudding.'

'Der in't no pudding,' Daisy said, putting in her spoke as ever.

'There is now, Daisy,' said Mrs Bagthorpe firmly. 'Tess has been shopping. Would you like some ice-cream?'

So the quartet made their way towards the house. As they did so, they were greeted by the combined sounds of drum and violin, and so did not notice muffled noises coming from the outhouse. (These were by now only half-hearted. Given the lack of windows, the pressmen had decided that they had better conserve oxygen, in case they were in for a long wait.)

Daisy unexpectedly produced a comb and tissue paper and began to blow tunelessly.

'Oh, bless her heart!' cried Mrs Bagthorpe. 'The child has made her own instrument!'

As a matter of fact, she had not. Some time ago, while William, Rosie and Tess were practising their instruments, Daisy had said jealously that *she* wanted to make nice music. Jack, who was there at the time, heard this with alarm. She had already pierced William's drum with a knife and fork, and Billy Goat Gruff had seriously trampled Rosie's fiddle.

'Come with me, Daisy,' he had said, 'and I'll give you something to play.'

She had initially been enchanted by the sound produced by the comb and paper, but had been distracted quite early on in her attempt to master her instrument, and had quite forgotten it till now. She followed the other three into the house, still buzzing away.

Tess had embarked on her career as chef by attempting to produce three elaborate dishes at the same time. The kitchen was a disaster area. Tess herself was wielding the electric blender.

'It won't stiffen!' she shrieked as the others entered. She was surrounded by empty eggshells and streaks of yolk. 'Why won't it stiffen?'

'Of course it will, eventually,' said Mrs Bagthorpe sensibly.

'I've been doing it ten minutes! Ten minutes!'

'I expect that you did not separate the eggs properly,' remarked Grandma.

Tess switched off the blender.

'What? What do you mean? I'm not stupid. The yolks are in there.'

She pointed to a basin. Grandma peered in.

'Broken,' she said. 'I expect some of the yolks became mixed with the whites.'

'Of course they did! What if they did?'

'Then the whites will never stiffen,' Grandma said. 'If the merest speck of yolk has got into them. Did you teach your children nothing, Laura?'

'It didn't say that in the recipe!'

'Of course not,' replied Grandma. 'It took it for granted that you would know.'

'Hell's bells and Dennis Potter! That's *that*, then,' said Tess bitterly, pushing away the blender. 'Bang goes the salmon mousse!'

'You could always make egg custard,' Grandma suggested.

'And stop her making that foul row!'

Daisy buzzed on heedlessly.

'This is Max, Tess dear,' said Mrs Bagthorpe, with terrible timing. 'Do you remember Tess, Max?'

'Perhaps *he* knows how to cook,' said Tess, ignoring the introduction. 'Someone had better. I'm through!'

She slammed out.

'Oh dear!' Mrs Bagthorpe looked round helplessly at the

uncooked ducks, the splattered eggs, and the general appearance of there having been a recent heavy fall of flour.

Jack came in.

'Crikey!' he said, impressed by the scene.

'Jack, dear, there you are,' said Grandma. 'Would you kindly reheat me some of that delicious-looking lasagne? I take it Tess did not make that? Nor yourself, Laura?'

'It's takeaway,' Jack told her.

'I have always said you lean too heavily on Mrs Fosdyke,' Grandma told her daughter-in-law. 'Now you are reaping the consequences.'

Mrs Bagthorpe was engaged in spooning out ice-cream for Daisy and Max, and managed to ignore this.

At this point there came the spurt of gravel that heralded the arrival of Uncle Parker. He and Aunt Celia entered just as Daisy and Max were sitting down to their dessert.

'Good grief!' exclaimed Uncle Parker, eyeing the devastation with respect. 'Fozzy done her nut and gone berserk, has she?'

'She's not here,' Jack told him. 'She's gone to a safe house.'

'Mrs Fozzy in prison,' remarked Daisy through her ice-cream. '*Everybody*'s in prison.'

'Dear child,' murmured Aunt Celia.

She had come to Unicorn House to share with her family the news of the forthcoming twins and the visitation. Uncle Parker had implored her not to.

'Think, dearest,' he had said. 'They will not understand. They are ordinary mortals, made of common clay.'

He had been particularly keen for Mr Bagthorpe not to hear of recent developments, and relieved not to see his car in the drive. Nor was there any sign of the two newspapermen he had directed there earlier.

'Sit down, Celia,' cried Mrs Bagthorpe hospitably, pushing forward a floury chair.

'Celia is pregnant, not an invalid,' Grandma said. 'There are

128

millions of us on this globe, and we are all here as a result of someone being pregnant.'

'Safe house, eh?' repeated Uncle Parker. He was keen to keep the conversation going on some other topic, in the hope that his wife would forget her reason for being there. He then saw Max.

'Hello,' he said, 'who's this?'

His first impression was much the same at his daughter's had been – that Max was in some way connected with the missing tramp. He was not, however, wearing a frock, and was clearly no substitute as a guru, with or without the Angel Factor.

'This is Max,' said Grandma. 'He and I are old friends.'

'It is Max Fosdyke, Russell.' Mrs Bagthorpe was taking fruitless swipes with a dishcloth at the spattered surfaces.

'Good Lord!' exclaimed Uncle Parker. 'So it is. How d'you do? Come to stand in for his ma, has he?'

'I have news,' murmured Aunt Celia.

'Henry not back yet?' inquired Uncle Parker, still beavering away at his distraction tactics. 'Haven't had the press round, have you?'

'Press?' cried Mrs Bagthorpe. 'Why?'

Uncle Parker had till now quite forgotten that she was supposed to be missing.

'Laura! You're back! My dear Laura – welcome!' He went forward and planted a kiss on her cheek.

'She has come back when it suited her,' said Grandma jealously. 'Having put us all through the torments of hell.'

'Well, yes,' he agreed. 'We were a touch concerned. Been anywhere interesting, Laura?'

'I have news,' said Aunt Celia again.

'She had been at Mrs Fosdyke's house,' Grandma told him. 'It was a ploy to get Stella Bright into the national news.'

Mrs Bagthorpe uttered a cry of protest at this calumny.

'I don't believe it,' said Uncle Parker. 'Now, if it had been Henry . . .'

'And how is dear Mr O'Toole?' Grandma asked. 'Albert has been asking after him.'

'Oh. Well. Spot of bother there, I fear. The old boy's legged it again. Not exactly legged it . . .'

He explained about the taxi-driver.

'Well I think it's good riddance,' Jack said. 'D'you want bread with your lasagne, Grandma?'

He was dubiously studying the loaf earlier piggled by Daisy.

'I have news,' said Aunt Celia plaintively.

'What *is* she talking about? said Grandma irritably. 'Pull yourself together, Celia.'

'You have already told us your news, Celia dear,' Mrs Bagthorpe told her. 'And we're all delighted for you and Russell.'

'Yes, we're pretty chuffed ourselves,' said Uncle Parker swiftly. 'What are you up to these days, Max?'

'He has come to stay with us for a few days,' said Mrs Bagthorpe, forestalling any reply. She was as keen for the world at large not to know about Max's little peccadillo as Uncle Parker was to prevent his wife spilling the beans about the Heavenly Twins and the Green-Eyed Angel.

'Really? Does Henry know?'

'Henry does not have the last word in this house,' said Grandma, who should know.

'Uncle Bag been in prison,' remarked Daisy. She pointed at Max. 'An' *he* been in prison.'

She meant the shed.

'Of course he hasn't!' cried Mrs Bagthorpe. 'Daisy has just been playing one of her little games,' she explained.

Daisy was now eyeing her mother. It was probably occurring to her that it was unfair that she should be on the loose.

'Come wiv me, Mummy,' she said. 'I dot somefing to show you. It outside.'

She went up and tugged at her mother's skirt. This was a welcome reprieve for Uncle Parker.

'Yes, why don't you, dearest? Get a spot of air.'

'I shall come with you,' said Grandma.

'Your lasagne's nearly ready,' Jack reminded her.

Aunt Celia rose and allowed herself to be led away by her daughter. Uncle Parker watched her go with mixed feelings. He was relieved that there was now no immediate danger of her telling her news, but worried about her reactions if Daisy led her anywhere near the pool with its ghastly occupants.

'Daisy's probably through with the pool now,' he told himself. He knew better than most that her threshold of boredom was low. He began to chirp up.

'So has Max come to cook while his ma's off?' he inquired.

If so, he had a very heavy hand with the flour.

'I been a cook,' said Max unexpectedly.

'Really?' cried Mrs Bagthorpe. She had not thought of Max as a person with Strings to his Bow.

'In the Navy.'

'Oh wonderful!'

She thought, positively, that the immediate Problem was solved. She had never been in the Navy herself, and knew no one who had. On the other hand, she had often heard of the marvellous food served up on cruise liners, with asparagus and lobsters, and elaborate puddings in the shape of fish or palm groves. The kind of food she was visualizing was very unlikely to be regulation fare for the crew of a clapped-out cargo boat.

And, when Max said he had been a cook, what he really meant was that he had for a time been assigned to galley duties. These had mainly comprised mincing vast quantities of meat for rissoles, chipping potatoes and cutting the stalks off cabbages. He had on occasion helped out with breakfast, and certainly knew how to frizzle sausages and heat up beans. He had also made toast, on the principle, 'If it's brown it's done, if it's black it's buggered'. He himself had no quarrel with this kind of diet, and in fact had thought the food the best part of

131

being in the Navy. (A psychologist would not have found this surprising. Just as the offspring of teetotallers drink like fish, and those of non-smokers smoke, so Max was bound to rebel against the exotic fare provided by his mother. For him, a meal of egg, chips and beans was a statement.)

At this point William entered and, like everyone else, was impressed by the state of the kitchen.

'Strewth!' he said. 'Been an explosion, has there?'

He was surprised to see Uncle Parker. He had imagined he would by now be holed up in The Knoll, besieged by the press.

'Tess has decided not to cook, after all,' his mother told him.

'So someone else had better shove those ducks in the oven and hope for the best,' he said. 'I'm not doing it.'

'No, dear, Max is. He is a trained chef.'

William brightened somewhat at this news. He personally hoped that he had not inherited a single trait from either of his own parents, but supposed it was possible that some of Mrs Fosdyke's genes were circulating in the puny frame of her son.

The telephone rang and William, as nearest to the door, went to answer it.

'What?' they heard him say. 'Who?' Then, 'How should I know? Hang on.'

He bawled through to the kitchen.

'Anyone seen a couple of reporters?'

'Of what, dear?' asked Mrs Bagthorpe. Uncle Parker held his peace.

'I certainly have not,' Grandma said. 'Though, if they wish to interview me, I am available.'

Max began to look like a cornered rabbit again.

'Sorry,' William said, and replaced the receiver.

'That was the *Sludge*,' he told everyone. 'Apparently a couple of their men have gone missing.'

'But why ever should they be here?' cried Mrs Bagthorpe naïvely.

William shrugged. He imagined that the missing men were the two he had dispatched earlier to The Knoll, and was not particularly keen for this fact to emerge in the presence of Uncle Parker.

'Says they made their last contact from a car phone, and they were on their way here to cover a story.'

At this, Max's eyes positively rolled. He looked ready to bolt. Grandma noted this.

'Your doing, I suppose, Laura,' she said. 'I hope you are now satisfied with all the vulgar publicity you have generated.'

Uncle Parker held his peace for much the same reasons as William. He rightly assumed that the missing men were the ones he had himself sent here, and realized that they were probably at this moment concealed in the shrubbery to the rear of the house, telephoto lenses at the ready. He frowned slightly as he remembered that his wife and daughter were out there somewhere, too.

'I'm getting really sick of all this,' Jack said. 'I just wish things would get back to normal.'

William gave a bitter laugh that he had certainly inherited from his father.

'Normal?' he echoed. 'What's normal?'

No one bothered to reply. For one thing, they probably did not know.

Eleven

Mr Bagthorpe, still at the Crown and Mitre, was by now seriously bored. He had rearranged the fittings of his room and done his shopping. He had eaten a lunch of steak and kidney pie washed down with beer. He went back to his room and had another stab at the crossword. The silence in there was oppressive. It was also alien. At Unicorn House, silence was unknown, unless in the dark reaches of the night (and not always then).

Mr Bagthorpe, though he would have denied this under torture, was missing his family. One way or another they kept his adrenalin flowing, his creative juices. He was now in a vacuum.

He paced restlessly about the room, had another go at opening a window (thereby radically bending a teaspoon from his self-service tray) and began morosely to consider reconnecting his radio. In the end he went out again, and his departure was duly clocked by the receptionist.

He strode down the High Street, fuelled by frustration and ready to pick a fight with anyone. Any policeman in his path would probably have had his hat knocked off.

'I could go home,' he told himself. He had not, after all, told his family he was going away, and would not therefore lose face by reappearing so soon. 'At least that all-fired tramp's gone.'

It was quite extraordinary that, at this very moment, he

should actually have set eyes on the all-fired tramp. Mr Bagthorpe was no believer in miracles, or even telepathy, but was none the less struck by this coincidence. He could hardly have invented a better one for one of his own plots.

Mr O'Toole appeared, unaccountably, to be haggling over fares with a taxi-driver. In Mr Bagthorpe's experience, tramps did not take taxis, they tramped.

'Look, mate,' the driver was saying, 'there's someone got to pay up. 'Arf the night all round the 'ouses – come on, get in.'

'I could do with a drink,' said Mr O'Toole amiably.

'You can 'ave a tubful when we get there, 'the driver told him. 'Unicorn 'Ouse, that's where we're going. And I don't leave till I'm paid.'

At this point he caught sight of another of yesterday's fares.

' 'Ere!' he exclaimed. 'You! You're Unicorn 'Ouse!'

The tramp turned, and at the sight of Mr Bagthorpe gave a wide, relieved, yellow-toothed smile.

'Bejam, if it isn't a small world!' he exclaimed.

'Not that small,' said the taxi-driver. 'Twenty miles round trip and extra for waiting and time-wasting.'

He was referring to the time spent at the station, filling in the police about the body in the bushes at The Knoll.

Mr Bagthorpe thought fast. His instinct was to argue. After all, the taxi had dropped himself and Jack off, and carried on with Uncle Parker and the tramp. He considered this a pretty watertight argument for Uncle Parker being liable for the fare. On the other hand he wanted to go home – but without the tramp. He had a blinding flash of inspiration.

'All right,' he said. 'How much? And I'll want a receipt.'

He could always bang it on to the sum already outstanding from Uncle Parker for the pool and goldfish.

'That was uncommon civil, sir,' said Mr O'Toole as the taxi drew off, 'and I'd buy you a drink if I had the ready.'

Mr Bagthorpe had plenty of drink. He had two full bottles of

Scotch in his wardrobe at the Crown and Mitre. Though not a noticeably thrifty man, he had bought an extra bottle because that particular brand was on offer. He was now glad he had done so. Mr O'Toole, he reflected, would probably need all this to put him out effectively. Moreover, if he could engineer the tramp up to his room it would guarantee that he would stay there, eventually senseless, while Unicorn House would become automatically a tramp-free zone. He was so struck by the beauty and simplicity of the scheme that he would have cried 'Eureka!' had he been that kind of man.

'Come on,' he said. 'I'll get you a drink.'

The tramp ambled obediently after him until they came to a standstill outside the Crown and Mitre. There, Mr Bagthorpe needed to do some more thinking. He had not noticed the receptionist's unusual interest in himself and his comings and goings. For a writer, he noticed very little. But he did know that most three-star hotels would not take kindly to seeing (and smelling) the likes of Mr O'Toole on their premises. In order to get the tramp across the lobby and into the lift there must clearly be some kind of distraction. It must be something sufficiently serious to get the receptionist out from behind her counter. Vague memories surfaced of stories about bombers being in the area. No self-respecting receptionist, he told himself, could ignore a bomb.

'Wait here!' he ordered, and strode back in for the umpteenth time that day, and straight over to the desk. So determined was his demeanour that the receptionist cowered, and measured with her eye the distance between herself and a handy copper warming-pan.

'Out there!' Mr Bagthorpe hissed. 'In the car park!'

'W-w-what?' she stammered.

'A man – planting a packet!'

'P-p-packet?'

'A bomb, fool! Get out there and look for yourself!'

The receptionist's eyes rolled, her mind went on freeze. Faced with the alternative of a mad-looking Mr Bagthorpe and a possible bomber, she chose the latter. Common sense was thrown to the winds. It did not even occur to her simply to pick up the phone and dial 999. She fled.

Mr Bagthorpe was back across the lobby in a flash. He unceremoniously grasped Mr O'Toole and began to propel him past the potted plants and brass toasting forks towards the lift. Luckily it was the post-prandial lull, and the place was deserted.

The lift was already on the ground floor, and Mr Bagthorpe shoved the tramp forward as the doors opened, then followed, pressing the button. In such close proximity to Mr O'Toole's far from fragrant person, Mr Bagthorpe thanked his lucky stars that this room was not on the twenty-first floor (which was not even a possibility, given that the Crown and Mitre was on only three floors). Mr O'Toole stood mildly gazing about him and blinking owlishly in the light. He had not been in a lift for years, and probably thought he was back in some kind of cell.

The door slid open.

'Come on – quick! Before they shut!'

Mr O'Toole obeyed with alacrity. He thought his host was referring to the bar, rather than the lift doors.

Moments later they were safely inside Mr Bagthorpe's room. Mr O'Toole gazed about him at the neat twin beds, the swagged curtains, the television set and trouser press. He was certainly not back in a Salvation Army hostel. On the other hand, there was no sign of a bar.

'Well,' he said politely, 'this is a fine place!'

'It's all yours,' Mr Bagthorpe told him. 'You're welcome to it.'

Still his guest stood looking uncertainly about him. He was at even more of a loss in such surroundings than Mr Bagthorpe himself. He was dimly aware that, whatever time it was, it was not bedtime. Mr Bagthorpe found his massive, moveless presence unnerving.

'Sit down!' He waved a hand.

Obediently Mr O'Toole sat on the end of one of the beds.

'Look,' Mr Bagthorpe said, 'this place is yours for the night. You've got your own bathroom – look!'

He held open the connecting door and the tramp gazed past him at the gleaming interior.

'You can have as many baths as you want. Here!' He fished in his pocket, took out the sachets of bath gel and tossed them over.

Still the tramp said nothing. Mr Bagthorpe's own social skills were not up to much at the best of times. On this occasion he found himself well and truly stumped. It did not seem to call for small talk, even if he had any. He despised small talk. If any unfortunate person chanced to remark on the weather, Mr Bagthorpe would raise his eyebrows. Sometimes he just walked away. Here, he had someone as little used to social chit-chat as himself. The silence could have gone on for ever.

Mr Bagthorpe detested silence. On a sudden inspiration he turned on the TV set – or tried to. It was a different make from the one at home, and all the buttons were in different positions. He pressed each one in turn, without result. He then traced the wire at the back of the set to the plug. It was not connected. He pushed in the plug, pressed the switch, then repeated the exercise with the knobs on the set. Nothing. All the while Mr O'Toole sat watching. This irritated the hell out of Mr Bagthorpe, who could not stand to be seen at a disadvantage.

'You try!' he snapped.

The tramp moved his head, looking about him. He then rose and lumbered to the bedside table. He picked up the remote control. Next moment a billiard table glowed from the screen. Mr Bagthorpe was thrown by this success, having not imagined that television sets abounded in hedgerows. He had never visited a Salvation Army hostel and knew nothing of the facilities there.

The tramp resumed his position at the end of the bed, and sat gazing at the screen, zapper in hand. Mr Bagthorpe went into the bathroom and picked up his new toiletries. He then fished in the waste bin and retrieved the discarded bags in which they had been wrapped. It occurred to him that the receptionist might smell a rat if she saw him leave clutching a toothbrush and paste.

'I'm off now,' he said. 'Here!'

He opened the wardrobe door, took out the bottles of Scotch and plonked them on top of the TV set.

'Glasses in the bathroom,' he said.

The tramp's eyes fixed on the bottles, his teeth showing yellow again.

'That's him sorted for the night,' Mr Bagthorpe told himself. He placed the room key by the bottles.

'I'll let myself out,' he said. 'Cheers!'

As he went he removed the Do Not Disturb sign, and hung it on the outside handle. Light of heart, he made for the lift and descended for the last time to the foyer.

'Oh – er – sir! Just a moment!'

He whipped round. It was the manager, with a still distraught-looking receptionist.

'Well?'

'Er – I understand – Miss Junior here – something about a suspicious package?'

'Look,' said Mr Bagthorpe, who had by now clean forgotten his earlier ruse, and had not foreseen its possible repercussions. 'If I thought there was a bomb in the place, would I have gone up to my room? Do I look like the kind of person who wishes to be blown apart and have his guts hanging on telephone wires?'

Put thus graphically, the answer had to be a clear negative. No one the manager could think of looked like that kind of person.

'But you said – '

'I merely said you can't be too careful.' Mr Bagthorpe knew there had been no witnesses. It was his word against the receptionist's.

'There have been rumours of bombers. As a good citizen, I simply mentioned a rum-looking character in the car park.'

He made an attempt to look like a good citizen.

'But there you are – I don't suppose anyone will thank me for it.'

He went on his way towards the swing doors.

'Er – thank you, thank you, sir!' called the manager after him.

He wished Mr Bagthorpe had never booked in at his hotel. He wished he would just get in his car and drive off and not come back. His wish was about to be granted but not, as he would eventually discover, without cost. Even then he did not fully appreciate the irony of his wish. He had never heard of, let alone read, *The Monkey's Paw* . . .

As Daisy led her mother into the garden her plan was clear. Earlier, there had been serious prison overcrowding. Now, the potting-shed was free again.

'You a bad mummy,' she told her unsuspecting parent.

Aunt Celia did not even hear this. She was gazing about her, having deep thoughts about the greenness and peacefulness of gardens.

'Der's lot of bad people,' Daisy continued. 'An' dey only gets crusses to eat.'

This, as a matter of fact, would not unduly have disturbed Aunt Celia even had she understood it. Although crusts did not figure high in her diet, she was probably the world's lightest eater. In a bid for this title she could probably have given Mahatma Gandhi a run for his money. She appeared to subsist on a diet of lettuce and spring water. Even now, she was certainly not eating for three.

140

'Is der a lickle stranger inside your tummy?' Daisy now suddenly demanded. It occurred to her that, if so, she had a bonus. She had an extra prisoner at a stroke.

Aunt Celia had certainly never told her daughter anything so crude. Has she troubled to say anything at all about the facts of life (about which she herself was rather vague) it would have been more on the lines of a Greek or Norse myth. It would have featured springing corn and mystical silver threads. Daisy would have grown up with very confused ideas about human reproduction.

Even as things were, she was hardly better informed. In response to repeated questioning by Daisy about the forthcoming lickle stranger, Grandma had attempted a rudimentary lesson. As she had never given her own children any sex education (and in turn had never been given any by *her* mother) she had not found this easy. Early on she had found herself floundering.

Grandma had kicked off by telling Daisy about chickens hatching from eggs. Daisy listened intently.

'Higgledy piggledy my black hen
 She lays eggs for gentlemen,' she nodded happily.

'Exactly!' cried Grandma. 'That's it in a nutshell!' (She meant eggshell.)

She mistakenly believed that the lesson was now over, but had reckoned without the penetrating logic of her granddaughter's mind.

'But Mummy *in't* no hen,' Daisy objected. 'She an't got no beak and she an't got no fevvers.'

Grandma was forced to concede that this was the case.

'But she is a kind of *human* hen,' she said.

Daisy shook her ringlets vigorously.

'She not!' she said emphatically. 'She don't lay no eggs.'

'Perhaps not as such . . .' conceded Grandma warily.

'I an't never seen her lay no eggs.'

'Ah, but you see, it's hidden,' Grandma had said incautiously. 'It's hidden in her tummy.'

At this Daisy's eyes had stretched.

'She dot a hen in her tummy?'

'No, no!' Grandma assured her hastily. She tried a different tack. 'Your mother is not going to have a chicken, she is going to have a baby.'

'I know,' nodded Daisy. 'She going to have a baby called Lickle Stranger, and I'm going to give it fings to eat and play dragons wiv it and so's Billy Goat Gruff.'

This seemed an uncertain future for any new-born baby, but Grandma made no comment. She thought, mistakenly, that the matter was now settled. She had, after all, fobbed off Aunt Celia with much the same kind of story.

'Where *is* der lickle stranger?' Daisy persisted.

'I told you, dear, it is in your mummy's tummy.'

Daisy was horror-struck. She was picturing babies as she knew them, complete with growsuits and frilly bonnets. She was, with inexorable progression, picturing herself in such a situation.

'But it can't breave!' she shrieked. 'Oh, poor lickle fing! Let it out, let it out!'

By now Grandma knew she had gone wrong somewhere.

'It *can* breathe, Daisy! she cried. 'It breathes like a fish!'

A new element had now been added to the already confused imagery of eggs and hens. Metaphors were well and truly mixed.

'Oo shall have a fishy
  On a lickle dishy,' said Daisy more or less automatically. The implications then sank in. Instead of a little brother or sister, it now seemed she was to have a fish.

'I want a baby I want a baby!' she screamed.

'It *is* a baby,' confirmed Grandma. 'It's swimming in mummy's tummy like a fish.' Any gynaecologist present would have shuddered.

142

'But oo knitting it a *bonnet*!' Daisy squealed. Even her fertile imagination balked at the picture invoked. 'Oo knitting it a bonnet an' a lickle black coat!'

She could evidently see the baby, thus kitted, fruitlessly swimming round and round somewhere under her mother's floating frock.

'Birth is a miracle,' said Grandma, hoping to ease the discussion into more philosophical and nebulous area.

As far as Daisy was concerned, a baby doing the backstroke in a black bonnet and matinée coat inside her own mother was a miracle too far.

'It not in der, it not!' she squealed.

'Let us play snakes and ladders,' suggested Grandma. 'Don't bother your little head about it.'

Daisy was not to be sidetracked by so obvious a ploy.

'Who put it der?' she demands.

'Your father, dear,' replied Grandma unwisely. She was now in real deep water. As soon as she had spoken she could have bitten off her tongue.

'Daddy?' Daisy was incredulous. 'Daddy's nice, he gives me choccies 'n Billy Goat Gruffs! What he do dat for?'

'It's what daddies do,' faltered Grandma, dreading the next question.

It came.

'How? How did Daddy put the lickle stranger in mummy's tummy?'

Grandma really was not up to this.

'It is one of life's great mysteries, Daisy dear,' she told her.

'Did you see him?' demanded Daisy.

'Well . . . no . . . not as such . . .'

'Den how you know he did it?' she asked triumphantly.

'I . . . we . . . I'm sure he did.'

'He din't he din't! It was dat nasty Uncle Bag! He's a nasty grockle an' *he* puts poor lickle babies in people's tummies!'

143

Grandma was aghast at the implications of this. She had unwittingly stirred up a real hornet's nest. While by and large she had little time for psychology, she could see that Daisy must on no account be left with this impression. It could mark her for life.

'Daisy, it was definitely your father,' she said firmly. 'If you wish, I will swear it upon the Bible.'

Daisy hesitated. She had seen her grandmother do this on previous occasions, and knew she took the matter seriously.

'Awright,' she said grudgingly at last. For the time being she would let the matter drop, but intended to tackle Uncle Parker later.

Grandma had accordingly fetched the Bible and sworn the paternity of the lickle stranger. She would have been severely miffed had she known that the whole charade was redundant, in that any baby inside Aunt Celia at present was strictly Phantom.

After the swearing ceremony Daisy put the whole matter on hold. Now it resurfaced. Her mother appeared not to hear her question, so she repeated it.

'Is der a lickle stranger in your tummy?'

'Oh Daisy,' murmured her mother, 'we are twice blest.'

' 'N did Daddy put it there?'

'Two precious, chosen souls, entrusted to my care!'

It was astonishing that Aunt Celia should believe that any souls she was likely to produce should be precious or chosen. It flew in the face of all previous experience.

'If he did, how he det it der?' persisted the indefatigable Daisy. 'Tummy buttons is only lickle. Did he post it in your mouf?'

These queries were falling on deaf ears. Aunt Celia was off somewhere on her own. She was a sitting duck for the potting-shed.

Daisy tugged her along, avoiding the pool, which she knew was not as attractive to her mother as it was to herself. Once at the potting-shed, she halted.

144

'Oo go in der,' she instructed her parent.

Aunt Celia gazed blankly through the open door.

'Oo go in der and shut your eyes 'n a surprise'll happen,' Daisy told her with perfect truth.

'But darling . . .' Aunt Celia protested feebly as her daughter started to push her in the required direction.

'It's mazic,' Daisy said. 'I been in der, and it's got all mazic fings.'

She knew, even without knowledge of the recent heavenly visitation, that magic went down very well with her mother. The enormous blue eyes turned wonderingly on those of her daughter.

'Oh Daisy . . . dearest . . . *you* have seen . . .?' She was a terrible judge of character. In four years, she had not remotely begun to sus Daisy. 'Have you . . . did you . . . an *angel*?'

'Oh ess,' said that child nonchalantly. 'I seen lots and lots. Dey in der.'

The huge eyes turned again to the dusty interior of the shed. To any ordinary mortal it did not even remotely resemble a grotto.

On the other hand, to Aunt Celia it did not even resemble a potting-shed. She did not know what a potting-shed was. To her, gardens were miraculous blessings of the universe, not places where people broke their backs and ruined their fingernails and dug and hoed and took cuttings and potted things in. To this extent, then, the shadowy interior of the shed represented a place of mystery, a possible sacred site.

'Go *on*!' said Daisy impatiently, and gave her mother another push.

Aunt Celia stepped in, hands clasped as if in supplication. Slam! The door was shut.

'Dot oo!' cried Daisy triumphantly.

Twelve

After her meal at the French restaurant Mrs Fosdyke's view of London mellowed perceptibly. There was certainly no food of that order (other than her own) to be had in her own neck of the woods. She therefore showed no resistance when Patsy Page suggested they should then go on a shopping expedition.

'Your outfit's terrific, Mrs F,' Ms Page told her, eyeing the turquoise polyester. 'But now you're in the public eye, you have to be at the leading edge of fashion.'

'Like Princess Di,' nodded Mrs Fosdyke happily.

It was hard to marry an image of that leggy lady with Mrs Fosdyke's own diminuitive and shapeless figure, but the reporter agreed vigorously.

'You'll be a knockout,' she assured her guinea-pig. At the very least, she could have a go at making her look something like the Queen Mother. She had no qualms about this. It did not occur to her that it was perhaps dangerous to tinker with someone's self-image, that geese turned into swans only in fairy-tales.

The reporter got on her mobile phone to request a photographer. She wanted every stage of Mrs Fosdyke's transformation to be recorded. Millions of readers out there would be identifying with her, seeing their own dreams acted out. (Given that those same readers daily checked their *Sludge* Bingo, believing themselves each time only one maddening number

146

away from a fortune, they were certainly hardened believers in dreams coming true.)

Ms Page was torn between making the first call to shops, or to the beauty salon. She shuddered at the thought of Mrs Fosdyke in her present guise entering the scented premises of the Knightsbridge hairdresser to the rich and famous. On the other hand, she was going to stand out like a sore thumb in the boutiques, too. She eventually plumped for the shopping. After all, if Mrs Fosdyke was wearing a rig-out whose cost ran into four figures, the staff could hardly sneer at her in the salon, however unmanicured her hands or radical her split ends.

'I can have a quick word with them while she's having her face steamed,' she told herself.

It was lucky for her that Mrs Fosdyke did not know that she was going to get steamed (and waxed, and vibrated and pummelled). She might easily have called the whole thing off.

The pair were driven to Knightsbridge and dropped off outside the boutique Ms Page had in mind.

'Ooh, there don't look much choice!' exclaimed Mrs Fosdyke, eyeing the three astronomically priced garments tastefully arranged in the window. Even inside, the place, though admittedly plush and well-chandeliered, was disappointingly bare. Mrs Fosdyke was used to rifling through rack upon rack of tightly packed garments at C & A or Littlewood's.

'You just take a look around while I have a word,' said Ms Page.

She held a whispered conference with a sales assistant who might have stepped straight out of *Dynasty*. That lady, who had frozen in horror at the sight of Mrs Fosdyke, now nodded sympathetically.

'And we might be able to give you a credit,' Ms Page told her. 'You know – hair by Frederick, gown by . . .'

This did not in fact appeal to the assistant, whose customers did not, by and large, favour the *Sludge*. Some of them had even

147

in the past been hounded by it, sued it for libel.

'There don't seem a lot in turquoise,' Mrs Fosdyke said, dubiously eyeing the creations about her. This was the shade she regularly favoured, though she sometimes called it duck-egg blue.

'Off with the old, on with the new!' cried Ms Page encouragingly.

She now realized that she should have taken her guinea-pig to Harrods first, for underwear. She dreaded to think what nether garments lay beneath the polyester, and would probably be revealed to the piercing eye of the saleslady. She would have been tempted to leave the shop had she known that Mrs Fosdyke ordered old-fashioned corsets from catalogues, and bought the rest of her underwear from market stalls.

'What about biscuit, madam?' The assistant indicated a pricey cream creation on a nearby stand.

'Looks a bit ordinary,' said Mrs Fosdyke, who did not go in for muted colours.

'I was thinking of madam's colouring,' said the assistant.

'Bring out your marvellous complexion,' added Patsy Page. 'Do try it!'

Mrs Fosdyke was ushered into a vast fitting-room lined with mirrors and her eyes flickered nervously at her own reflection. As she took off her best suit and laid it on a padded velvet chair she tried hard not to look up at her own corsets.

The cream two-piece fitted perfectly, she could tell that, even as she fiddled with hooks and buttons. Also, it felt delicious, soft and slippery against her skin, unlike anything she had ever worn before. She raised her eyes and looked bravely into the glass and actually gave a little gasp.

She was already transformed. Even with her frizzy hair, thick stockings and sensible shoes, there was an indefinable some-thing about her appearance that Mrs Fosdyke recognized and approved.

'Ooh!' she said to herself. 'I look like a real lady!'

She emerged, bashful and proud, awaiting reaction.

'Wonderful!' enthused Ms Page. 'You look a million dollars, Mrs F!'

'It is certainly madam's style,' said the assistant, who was keen to get Mrs Fosdyke off the premises as soon as possible, before any of her regular clients appeared. 'In fact, it could have been made for her.'

It had in fact been made for a well-known actress who had been run over by a bus before she could collect it.

'I'll take it!' said Mrs Fosdyke happily.

'Keep it on,' Ms Page urged. 'Then we can go and choose accessories to match.'

Mrs Fosdyke needed no persuading. Her whole being responded to the look and feel of the thing; she seemed to feel herself grow inches taller. She was still in a dream as her minder propelled her from the shop.

'Harrods!' she cried.

Mrs Fosdyke did not even protest, convinced as she was that Harrods was a daily target for bombers. She was persuaded into shoes with high heels, and fine denier tights. Bag and gloves were bought to match. While Mrs Fosdyke was left in Lingerie to select underclothes, Patsy Page chose a tasteful brooch with matching earrings. She was not very observant for a reporter, or she would have noticed that Mrs Fosdyke's ears were not pierced.

Back in the car and on their way to the hairdresser's Ms Page presented Mrs Fosdyke with the jewellery. First came the brooch.

'Ooh, it's like Christmas!' cried Mrs Fosdyke, and pinned it on. 'Ooh – and earrings! Ooh, you've bought the wrong kind! I only wear clip-ons, you know.'

Just then the car drew up and Ms Page was prevented from learning why Mrs Fosdyke's ears had not been pierced.

'Probably got another of her half-baked theories about *that*,' she thought.

The *Sludge* photographer was waiting outside the salon, and Mrs Fosdyke was happy to pose for him, though she was still a little unsteady on the high heels. He clicked wearily away. He couldn't see what the fuss was about. Where he came from, the likes of Mrs Fosdyke grew on trees, and as a rule he avoided them like the plague. She struck him as a far cry from Eddie the Eagle.

'Bet she can't even ski,' he thought.

Once inside the salon Ms Page held a discreet word with the owner while Mrs Fosdyke looked nervously about her. She had rarely before entered any hairdressing salon, let alone an establishment such as this. Herself and Mesdames Pye and Bates had formed a kind of cooperative, and generally did home perms on one another in their own kitchens.

'Right, Mrs F – I've given instructions for you to have the full works,' Ms Page told her. 'I'll leave you in Frederick's capable hands while I just nip into the office. Oh – and you won't forget the ear-piercing, will you?'

'The what?' said Mrs Fosdyke, overhearing this aside.

'You'll surely want to wear the beautiful earrings?'

'I only wear clip-ons,' said Mrs Fosdyke doggedly.

'Oh, it won't hurt, I assure you,' said Frederick, smiling.

'I dare say,' said Mrs Fosdyke sourly. 'And what about Aids?'

The word dropped like a brick into that scented air. One or two of the heads were already turning.

'All our equipment is absolutely sterile madam,' said Frederick stiffly. 'This is not a back-street tattooist.'

'Tattoos?' shrieked Mrs Fosdyke. She turned and tottered towards the door, but Ms Page caught her by the arm.

'Of course not,' she said soothingly. 'That was just Frederick's little joke. Not your style at all.' She herself had a green butterfly on her left shoulder. 'A discreet look – a mature elegance.'

This sounded better. Also, Mrs Fosdyke had now sighted

some of the other clients, and was forced to admit they did look good. She did rather hanker for a similar look herself.

'Oh, all right, then,' she agreed. 'But – no needles!'

If Mrs Fosdyke could have seen the state of her kitchen at around that time, she would probably have given her notice and opted to stay in London for ever. It was by now deserted. The younger Bagthorpes were holed up in their rooms, Uncle Parker had joined Grandpa watching television, and Grandma was having a second stint at her memoirs. She had departed in moderate dudgeon after Mrs Bagthorpe had taken Max off to her den.

'I shall counsel you,' she told him, 'and instruct you in the rudiments of Positive Thinking.'

'That has not done *you* much good, Laura, in the past,' Grandma told her. 'I think I should counsel Max. I have far greater experience of life.'

This was unarguable. But Mrs Bagthorpe was fired with missionary zeal. She was hell-bent on saving Max from himself.

'Do not forget that I am Stella Bright,' she told her mother-in-law. 'And a magistrate. My experience of human nature goes far beyond the narrow confines of family life. Come, Max.'

He went, not without misgivings. In her crowded little den Mrs Bagthorpe seated herself at her desk and invited him to take a seat opposite.

'Now Max,' she began, 'I know that at this moment you are racked with remorse for your crime, and cast down in the depths of despair.'

This was not at all the case. Max had not committed murder. He had obtained a measly fifty pounds from a purloined cash card. What was weighing on his mind was not his crime, but the possibility of being pulled in for it. He couldn't help feeling that he was in the worst possible place. Pressmen and police seemed to be drawn to the Bagthorpes as moths were to a flame.

'I expect that the first thing you would wish to do is to repay the money,' Mrs Bagthorpe continued. 'This is very important.'

'But I ain't got fifty quid. That's why I took it in the first place,' he pointed out.

'I understand that. But once you are in gainful employment you will soon be able to save such a sum.'

'What employment?' Max asked.

'A very simple solution has occurred to me,' she told him. 'Your mother is at present away from home. I don't expect she will be back for at least a week. For that period, her situation is vacant.'

This seemed self-evident. Max still did not see what she was driving at.

'Now, you have been in the Navy. I expect you like things to be shipshape and Bristol fashion.' She smiled. 'Also, as you have already told us, you are a chef.'

'Not exactly a chef,' he mumbled.

'Perhaps not a qualified chef,' Mrs Bagthorpe agreed. 'But then, nor is your mother, and she is a simply wonderful cook. What I am saying is that *I* will employ you to carry out her duties. What do you say to that?'

Max's reaction to this offer was cool. If she had expected to be showered with effusive thanks, and assurances of devotion to duty, she was disappointed. When Mrs Fosdyke described her son as a long-haired layabout, she had been right on both counts. Once Mrs Bagthorpe had tidied him up, he would become a short-haired layabout.

Work was not a word in Max's vocabulary. He had left the Navy as soon as he discovered that life was not the non-stop pleasure cruise to tropical parts he had imagined. His ideal life would be to stay in bed for the best part of the day, then sit far into the night with a six-pack of lager, watching videos. Mrs Bagthorpe's offer came as a severe shock. Unicorn House was large and would need a lot of cleaning. He felt extremely stressed. His reaction to this was not to take the Deep Breaths that Mrs Bagthorpe herself would have recommended.

'I don't suppose you've got a fag?' he asked.

It was now a full twenty-four hours since he had last had one.

'A f – a *cigarette*?' said Mrs Bagthorpe in shocked tones. 'Max!'

Unicorn House was a strictly smoke-free zone. Each of the young Bagthorpes had been promised two hundred pounds if it reached the age of twenty-one without succumbing to the habit. Unknown to their mother, the three eldest had already tried it and pronounced it disgusting. Jack had actually been sick.

'That decides the matter,' Mrs Bagthorpe said firmly. 'While you are under this roof there will be no smoking. We shall kill two birds with one stone. By the end of the week you will be able to repay your debt, and will have freed yourself from a disgusting and life-threatening habit.'

She then went on to lecture him on the benefits of Deep Breathing and Positive Thinking. She gave him to understand that if he practised these faithfully, there was nothing he could not achieve. He could probably be Prime Minister, if he wanted to, or Poet Laureate.

'Your self-esteem is very low, Max,' she told him. 'The very fact that you are putting your health at risk by smoking is proof enough. Now tell me – what is your Life Plan?'

'My what?'

'Where do you wish your life to go? What are your dreams?'

Max racked his brains. He had never thought of himself as having a career. His main concern was to get from one day to the next.

'It'd be nice to win the pools,' he offered.

'I don't agree, Max,' she told him. 'Your object in life is to develop your full potential. Who knows what gifts lie latent? You must not hide your light under a bushel.'

He had not the foggiest idea what she was talking about.

'All right,' he said, thinking this a safe response.

'Splendid!' she cried. 'Now – shoulders back, spine straight! You cannot Breathe if you slouch. That's better! Now – a deep, deep Breath! No – using your whole lungs – right from the diaphragm. And hold . . . and out! Again . . .'

Max kept making loud sniffing noises in the hope that these would pass as Deep Breathing. He could not seem to get the hang of it at all. The more he thought about it, the harder it became. He began to be frightened that he might stop breathing altogether.

'Wait! I know! I have a book. Wait here and practise, and I will fetch it.'

Mrs Bagthorpe left Max sniffing and hurried downstairs. She had for years been urging her husband to take up Breathing, which might at least, she hoped, improve his temper. Recently she had lent him a manual on the subject and this, she guessed, would be in his study. This room was now regularly locked to prevent further incursions by Daisy. Mrs Bagthorpe had prudently had a nail for the key placed at a height well out of that infant's reach.

Now, using it, she let herself in. It seemed eerily quiet and empty in there. The waste bin was filled to overflowing, a poignant indication of creative failure. As a rule, Mrs Bagthorpe respected her husband's privacy, as she expected him to respect her own. She felt like an intruder. She found the book lying on a pile of junk catalogues and retreated hastily, quite forgetting to lock the door behind her. Across the hall she could hear the television. She peered in and saw Grandpa and Uncle Parker, both asleep.

'Bless them!' she told herself more or less automatically.

She gently closed the door and went back upstairs to resume the tutorial.

No sooner had she gone than Daisy appeared with Billy Goat Gruff in tow. After incarcerating her mother she had run across him polishing off pansies in one of the borders.

'Oo a naughty boy,' she told him severely. 'Oo dot to go to prison.'

She was up against prison overcrowding again. There was a shortage of places with keys to turn and throw away. For her, then, it seemed something of a miracle to come across a door complete with key.

'Der's a prison!' she cried.

It was no easy matter to get her prisoner inside. Billy Goat Gruff had not had a proper meal since he had demolished Aunt Celia's boudoir. He evidently liked the smell of Italian that was still emanating from the kitchen. He pulled that way, Daisy tugged the other. In the end he gave up. He probably knew Daisy as well as anyone ever could, and had by now worked out that she had the tenacity of a pit bull terrier, and the staying power of the Great Wall of China.

With her free hand Daisy turned the handle of the study door, then dragged her pet inside after her.

'This in't no real prison,' she told him, 'cos it an't got no dudgeons and spiders. You jus' stop here and be sorry.'

The goat looked about him with calm yellow eyes.

'I might bring you a cruss,' she continued. 'All you get is crusses and water.'

Seemingly unmoved by this threat, the goat wandered over to the waste bin. This did not escape the sharp eyes of his keeper.

'No! *Dat*'s not crusses!' She ran and picked up the bin and plonked it squarely on Mr Bagthorpe's desk. Then she left, locking the door behind her.

'Lock him up and *frow* away the key!' she chanted as she did so. 'Lock the door and *frow* away der key!'

Off she pranced, out of the house and away down the drive, in search of a suitable thicket.

'Lock him up and *frow* away der key! Lock him up and *frow* away der key – eeech!'

There was a screech of brakes, a spurt of gravel. She had narrowly missed being run over by Mr Bagthorpe, who now sat glaring and cursing behind the wheel. Daisy was no less furious. She ran straight at the car and delivered a hard kick, then another.

'Oo look out oo look out!' she screamed.

Mr Bagthorpe's jaw dropped. He sat helpless under the onslaught.

'What oo *do*? I nearly got runned over!'

He sincerely wished that this had been the case. It would have been as neat a murder as anyone could have hoped for, and might not even have attracted a charge of manslaughter.

'I could say she ran straight out in front of me!'

He revved his engine threateningly, but Daisy held her ground.

'Oo's a bad man! Why oo not in prison?'

'Clear off!' he yelled, and pressed his hand on the hooter.

Daisy now began to jump up and down with fury, and seemed to have plenty to say, though this was mercifully drowned by the blare of the horn. Grimly he kept his hand on it. After what seemed an age Daisy gave a final stamp, stuck out her tongue and scampered off into the bushes.

Mr Bagthorpe proceeded up the drive, cursing. As he reached the final bend he saw Uncle Parker's scarlet roadster parked in front of the house. This, he thought, was all he needed.

He entered the house, which seemed uncannily quiet. The only sounds seemed to be coming from the sitting-room, where the door stood ajar. Above the background noise of the television he recognized the voices of Jack and Uncle Parker. Mr Bagthorpe was not above eavesdropping. He went right up to the door and listened.

'I still don't get it,' Jack was saying. 'Is she expecting twins, or isn't she?'

'She's expecting twins, all right,' said Uncle Parker gloomily. 'Trouble is – how'll she react when they don't materialize.'

'Won't they even be Phantoms, then?'

'Look, Jack,' said Uncle Parker. 'It's the *pregnancy* that's Phantom. What that means is that she won't be getting anything.'

'So why does she think she will?'

'Search me,' replied Uncle Parker, with entire honesty. 'But she's got it firmly fixed in her head that she's expecting twins, and, to cap it all, she's now seen an Angel.'

'A what?'

Mr Bagthorpe congratulated himself on picking up more ammunition than he could have dared hoped for. He listened, smirking, as his adversary described Aunt Celia's visitation.

'But she can't really have seen one,' Jack objected.

'Seems so. Even got the colour of its eyes. Green, she says.'

Mr Bagthorpe judged the moment propitious to make his entrance.

'Did I hear right?' he said.

The pair of them jumped.

'So Celia has finally fallen right out of her tree,' he went on. 'Green-Eyed Angels, eh? And Phantom Twins. I congratulate you, Russell.'

'It is entirely possible that Celia has seen an Angel,' replied Uncle Parker, keeping his cool. 'If any mortal should be privileged to see one, it is undoubtedly herself.'

'Amen to that,' returned Mr Bagthorpe. 'By now your place is probably swarming with them. Still, better than twins, eh?'

'You are not to say a word about this to Celia,' Uncle Parker warned. 'She is in a very delicate condition.'

'As ever,' said Mr Bagthorpe. 'Are you serious? Someone's got to warn her. Does Laura know? Does Mother?'

'No one knows,' said Uncle Parker. 'And I suggest you forget you ever heard it.'

157

'Phantom Twins, eh?' mused Mr Bagthorpe. 'That's a turn-up for the books. Make medical history, I shouldn't wonder.'

At this point there came a diversion.

'Crikey!' Jack exclaimed. He ran to the television and turned up the volume. 'Look at her!'

It really was surprising that Jack had recognized her at all. With her beautifully coiffed hair and cream silk, she looked for all the world like a Conservative cabinet minister, or a dowager duchess. It was probably the way she was clutching her handbag that gave her away.

'. . . captured the imagination of the nation . . .' the interviewer was saying.

'Good grief!' exclaimed Mr Bagthorpe in disgust. 'What's that woman doing on the box?'

'In the case of Hannah of the Dales, such a character came to light through a television documentary. Gladys Fosdyke leapt into the headlines after a bomb incident in her own home. Most women would have been traumatized by such a thing. But Gladys took the whole thing in her stride. Tell me, what was the worst moment?'

'Ooh, it was seeing that bomber through me own front window,' Mrs Fosdyke replied. ''Orrible scruffy thing!'

'The invasion of the sanctity of your own home . . .'

'Ooh yes,' nodded Mrs Fosdyke. 'He was stood there as if 'e owned the place. I nearly dropped dead on the spot. I've got a nervous breakdown, you know. Mainly on account of the lunatics I work for. Would you believe I found a bucket of dead goldfish in my own pantry?'

'However did that happen?' gasped the interviewer, quite forgetting the terrorist and the bomb.

'You'd better listen to this, Russell,' said Mr Bagthorpe.

'Overdose of milk,' said Mrs Fosdyke simply.

'Milk?' queried the interviewer faintly.

'She'd tried to bring 'em round with brandy, but it's my belief they was already dead when they was put in that bucket. 'Arf a pint of my cooking brandy!'

'Could we perhaps start at the beginning, Gladys?' said the interviewer, trying to remember her training.

So Mrs Fosdyke started at the beginning, with the rows of milk bottles lining the drive of Unicorn House on their return from the ill-fated visit to Wales. Enough to make custard to feed an army, she said, or rice pudding for the nation. She proceeded to a character assassination of Daisy Parker. She listed past misdemeanours. The viewers were given Billy Goat Gruff drunk on whisky, fire and flood, a string of funerals and finally the slaughter of innocent goldfish.

Your average viewer was doubtless riveted by all this. Not so Mr Bagthorpe. She was dragging the name of Bagthorpe through the mud, he fumed. He began to talk of writs for libel.

'Facts, dear Henry, facts,' drawled Uncle Parker. He seemed unfazed by the dragging of his own daughter's name through the mud. 'Hardly recognize the old bat, would you? Can't see her scrubbing your floors in that outfit.'

To this Mr Bagthorpe replied that if she were to do any scrubbing of floors it would be in Holloway Prison, to which Uncle Parker replied that libel, even if proved, did not involve a gaol sentence.

'Just filthy lucre,' he said, 'and I should doubt she can lay her hands on much of that. If you must sue, sue someone with a spot of the ready. The *Sludge* is a fair bet.'

At this point they all became aware of sounds that were not emanating from the television set. They were sounds of banging and crashing, and they seemed to be coming from across the hall.

'My God! The goat!' Mr Bagthorpe ran out and tried the handle of the study door. It did not budge. From within came the unmistakable sound of devastation. He wrenched at the handle and at the same time looked up to the nail where the key

159

usually hung. It was empty. Daisy was not in there, as he knew. In his agitated state it seemed to him that the only possible conclusion was that the goat had locked itself in there.

'I am going mad,' he told himself, horrified. 'This time, I am definitely going mad.'

Like Job, he felt that his fortunes were now at their nadir. He was, of course, wrong.

Thirteen

'You all right, Ken?' Bill asked in a hoarse whisper.

'Yeah. Really happy,' returned his colleague sourly.

Neither of them knew how long they had been incarcerated, nor how long the oxygen would last out. They did not know why they were there. They did not know how, if they got out alive, they were going to explain things to the editor.

As newsmen, they knew that the nation was going to the dogs, and that one clear sign of this was the increase of juvenile crime. They had covered plenty of stories involving break-ins by nine-year-olds, and teenage joyriders. This, however, was something else again. What was more, they were on the receiving end of it.

Each had silently pondered on what might be their eventual fate. They had both thought a lot about Daisy herself. She looked almost preternaturally innocent, with her large blue eyes and golden ringlets. But there had definitely been something spooky about her. That goat, for a start, got up like a Christmas tree. The Goats, they reminded themselves nervously, were associated with the devil. Then they remembered the pool, and the bloated fish in the saucepan. Some kind of ritual had evidently been going on. Then there was the matter of the deep-freeze and Stella Bright's body. If it really was in there, who had dispatched her and put it there? And how did that child know? Why was she not upset, as any normal four-year-old would have been? She had seemed absolutely matter-of-fact about the whole thing. It was uncanny. They were beginning, after hours of silence and darkness, to mythologize her.

They were even beginning to visualize the headlines in their own newspaper when their bodies were eventually discovered. They tried hard not to, they tried to push the picture away, but horrible alliterative phrases kept recurring. Both began to make resolutions about how, if they were miraculously found alive, they would try to lead better lives. They promised that they would never again camp for days on end on innocent people's doorsteps. They would renounce the use of the telephoto lens and quit bending the evidence in the interests of a snappy headline. If such reforms led to their being dismissed from their jobs, so be it.

'Think they've missed us at the office yet?'

Neither knew. They had originally been assigned to the Knaresborough Knifer story, but seemed to have come a long way since their vigil outside Aysham Police Station. They had encountered an unhinged woman claiming heavenly visitations, a pool full of dead fish, a decorated goat and finally their captor. None of this in itself seemed headline material, yet the cumulative effect had been to give both men a powerful sense of dissociation from the real world, of being caught up in something beyond any previous experience.

'At least you made that phone call,' Ken said. 'They'll know where we are.'

Had they known it, a second news- and cameraman had already been dispatched by the *Sludge* editor.

'Don't come back till you've found 'em,' they were told. 'Is this Unicorn place a pub, d'you think?'

Those same newsmen were cautiously approaching Unicorn House just as Mr Bagthorpe discovered that Billy Goat Gruff was locked in his study. After vainly wrenching at the handle he then ran out of the house with the intention of looking in through the study window to see what was going on. He did not even notice the advancing pressmen who, after exchanging looks, went after him. He looked like a man on the point of committing murder and, as such, was a possible scoop.

They turned the corner of the house to see Mr Bagthorpe banging on the study window and yelling out a stream of imprecations and threats. These contained a lot of references to someone called Daisy who, they supposed, was his intended victim. With any luck, this Daisy would open the window and Mr Bagthorpe would dispatch her under their very noses, and they could get a picture of this.

Mr Bagthorpe could, if he wished, have picked up a stone, broken a pane and climbed in to deal with the goat. This was what he would have liked to do, but cowardice prevented him. He genuinely did believe that Billy Goat Gruff was a killer, and had no wish to end up impaled on his horns. His dancing up and down and uttering threats were simply his way of letting off his feelings, rather than any real expression of intent. He carried on so long in this vein that in the end the pressmen went up behind him and peered past him through the window.

What they saw was Billy Goat Gruff in classic destruction mode. He was making runs at everything, head down, and even as they watched an anglepoise lamp went flying, followed in quick succession by a half-empty bottle of Scotch.

They gaped. In their experience, goats were either in fields or tethered by ropes and cropping verges. Neither had ever seen one inside a house. Nor had they seen one festooned in ribbons and bows.

Like their colleagues, they made the connection between the goat and the devil. They nervously wondered whether Mr Bagthorpe's cleared desk was some kind of altar. As they did so, a further sinister ingredient was added, a horrible, high-pitched screeching from somewhere overhead. Grandma, realizing that her son had returned, was bringing the Valkyries into play.

An upper window opened, and the newsmen craned up to see

an elderly lady peering down at them.

'Goods afternoon,' she called above the din. 'Are you plain-clothes policemen? Have you come to arrest Henry?'

It was only then that her enraged son realized he was not alone. He whirled round and glared so fiercely that they dropped back several paces. For all they knew, they were face to face with the dreaded Knaresborough Knifer. (So far, all his victims had been female, but there was no law to say serial killers should be consistent.)

'Who the devil are you?' he demanded. 'What are you doing on my property? Clear off!'

They were tempted to do so. But a couple of their colleagues had gone missing on a visit to this place, and they thought they were beginning to see why. Mr Bagthorpe turned his attention to his mother. 'And you can cut that out!' he bawled, meaning the Valkyries.

'I have no idea what you are talking about, Henry,' she replied. 'Why are you behaving like a madman?'

'I *am* a madman!' he yelled. 'I'm mad mad mad!' He kicked at the wall with each repetition, and the newsmen flinched. 'Who put that bloody goat in my study? Where is she? I'll throttle her!'

'Don't be silly, Henry,' Grandma told him. 'The goat is perfectly harmless.'

'Harmless? Harmless?' His voice went sliding up the scale at a pitch that mingled horribly with the massed voices of the Vienna State Opera Company.

Grandma's head disappeared. Almost simultaneously Mrs Bagthorpe came hurrying round the corner of the house.

'Henry!' she cried. 'What a dreadful noise! What has happened!'

'I'll tell you what's happened,' he said through gritted teeth. 'That bloody child has let that bloody goat loose in my study again, that's what's happened!'

164

'Language, Henry,' she murmured, directing an apologetic look towards the pressmen, who could have given anybody lessons in swearing. Then, 'But, however . . . oh, she must have stood on a chair to get the key!'

She, too, peered in through the window. Billy Goat Gruff was still firing on all cylinders.

'Oh dear . . .' she murmured. She turned to the pressmen. 'And who – '

'Tony Wyman, the *Sludge*, madam.' He flashed a press card.

'The *what*?' Mr Bagthorpe's face suddenly suffused alarmingly; he seemed about to have a seizure. He had no objections in principle to this notorious rag and its reporting methods. It was its TV critic he had it in for. This luminary turned out headlines like BAGTHORPE BOOBS AGAIN and had told his readers that he was unable to report on Henry Bagthorpe's latest offering for the simple reason that he had fallen asleep only ten minutes into it. The piece had been headed THE SNORE FACTOR.

'But – why are you here?' asked Mrs Bagthorpe. 'We have no news.'

'They don't *print* news,' gritted her husband. 'Out! Out!'

'I will speak with you in a moment,' Mrs Bagthorpe told them, 'after I have dealt with the goat. Daisy really is naughty.'

With this serious understatement she hurried off with the intention of unlocking the study door and releasing Billy Goat Gruff. Her husband strode after her.

'There's no key!' he yelled. 'The bloody key's gone.'

'They're nutters,' murmured Tony Wyman, beginning to wish himself in Bosnia, or the Gaza Strip.

In the hall Grandma, Jack and Uncle Parker were already gathered, listening to the crashing and banging coming from the study and gazing at its keyless keyhole.

'Oh!' Mrs Bagthorpe herself now saw this.

165

'Told you!' Mr Bagthorpe told her. 'Where were you?' he demanded of the others. 'Where were you when that accursed infant stole my key?'

'You can't actually *hear* someone stealing a key,' Jack pointed out, reasonably enough.

'There is no chair,' murmured Mrs Bagthorpe, measuring with her eye the height of the nail that had held the key. 'So how . . .?'

Then she remembered. She was utterly without guile. Any sensible person would have omitted to mention a visit to the study that no one could have suspected or detected. Her hand flew to her mouth.

'Oh dear!' they all looked at her. 'It – I'm afraid – you see, I was looking . . .'.

'You are rambling, Laura,' Her husband told her. 'Spit it out!'

She drew a deep breath.

'I went into the study earlier,' she said bravely. And I think I must have – '

'You? *You?* You let that goat in there?'

'No, no, of course not! I merely – forgot to lock the door.'

' "Merely," she says,' said Mr Bagthorpe bitterly. 'I suppose she thinks terrorists merely happen to leave bombs under cars, and lightning merely strikes people dead. There's nothing mere about what's going on in there!'

He kicked the study door.

'Aren't you overreacting a touch, Henry?' drawled Uncle Parker. 'After all, we've all had to learn to live with the goat.'

'He doesn't live here!' shouted Mr Bagthorpe. 'He lives at your place. Why isn't he there destroying that!'

Uncle Parker did not mention the goat's earlier activities in the nursery and the bower. To do so would be to supply his adversary with further ammunition.

'I'm going to buy a gun and learn to shoot it!' Mr Bagthorpe announced. 'And I advise you to do the same. You've got

166

enough on your plate with Phantom Twins and Angels, without – ' he broke off. He grinned. Now was his moment. 'Did you know, Mother, did you know, Laura, that Celia isn't expecting a baby?'

'Of course she is,' said Mrs Bagthorpe. 'She told us so herself.'

Mr Bagthorpe grinned again, and beckoned to the newsmen, who stood nervously by the door.

'A word,' he said. 'I've got a story for you!'

Max, who had been in the kitchen with Mrs Bagthorpe when her husband discovered the goat in his study, heard these words. He was tempted to bolt back to the safety of the shed. On the other hand, he reminded himself, Mr Bagthorpe was not yet aware of his presence in Unicorn House. He decided to make a start on clearing the mess made by Tess, then set about preparing the evening meal.

He was under the table mopping up flour and egg when Daisy trotted in through the back door. He straightened up, and she recognized him at once.

'Oo's dat naughty man dat was in prison with Grandma Bag!' she told him reproachfully.

'Sshh!' The very mention of the word 'prison' made him nervous.

'What's your name? I'm Daisy Parker and I'm four and I can kill people wiv death rays!'

'Oh yeah?' returned Max. 'I'm Max Fosdyke and I eat little girls for dinner.'

If he thought this threat would send her running straight out again he was disappointed. There were few things Daisy was afraid of, and she was a surprisingly good judge of character. She had already made a lightning assessment of Max, with his puny frame and nervous, flicking eyes, and had him down as an inadequate.

'I jus' frowed away the key,' she told him. 'I locked the door and frowed away the key!'

She had in fact thrown two keys. When she had thrown away the key to Mr Bagthorpe's study she had remembered the earlier key. When she had locked the newsmen in the outhouse she had certainly tossed it away then and there, and had enjoyed doing so. But it had fallen only a few yards away, and she now thought it should be thrown where it was less likely to be found. She accordingly trotted back, fetched it and threw it after the other.

Max had not the foggiest idea what Daisy was talking about, and in any case had not the least interest in having a conversation with her. He decided to ignore her.

As a tactic, this was a non-starter. Daisy was unignorable. She did not even register that she was being ignored. She followed Max about the kitchen, burbling about this and that, and getting on his nerves. He noticed that, in the hall, there was sudden quiet. The shouting had stopped and the only sounds were the occasional muffled thump or crash from the study. Even the sound of musical instruments being furiously practised had stopped. The house seemed all at once deserted.

Max, despite Mrs Bagthorpe's counselling, was by no means already a reformed character. It occurred to him that if he nipped upstairs he might find some valuables he could flog, or even money. (He had already automatically opened most tins and boxes in the kitchen and peered hopefully in.)

'You live here?' he asked Daisy, abandoning his failed tactic.

'Dat nasty Uncle Bag lives here,' she told him. 'I live with my mummy and my daddy and Billy Goat Gruff an' Arry Awk.'

This was disappointing news. Max had hoped she might point him in the direction of any valuables. He was not above using a four-year-old as an accomplice.

Daisy had in fact temporarily forgotten the invisible Arry Awk. Now that her other friend had been locked up and the key thrown away, it seemed a good time to resurrect him.

'Arry Awk's a naughty boy,' she confided. 'He makes all fires and floods.' Her eyes brightened at the memory.

168

'Oh yeah?' returned Max. 'And how old's he, when he's at home?'

'Oh, he in't any old,' Daisy assured him. 'He jus' Arry Awk. What you doing wiv dose poor dead hens?'

'Ducks,' corrected Max. He was weighing them pensively in each hand. He put them down again.

'Ducks!' squealed Daisy. 'Ducks are a-dabbling up tails all!'

'Not now, they're not,' said Max heartlessly. He had a vague idea that ducks were meant to be roasted with oranges stuffed up them, but decided to dispense with the frills. He turned the oven on high and began to hunt for a roasting tin.

'Poor lickle dead ducks.' Daisy stood prodding at their mottled flesh with her chubby forefinger.

Max now picked up a recipe book and began to study it. This required extreme concentration. He had left school with a reading age of about seven, and by now could hardly remember the alphabet. It was lucky that ducks were to be roasted, rather than swans or widgeons, or he would have become hopelessly bogged down in the index. As it was, he found the 'D's without too much trouble, and ran his finger slowly down them, past Dab and Dark Thick Orange Marmalade, through Devilled Crab and Doughnuts by way of Dublin Bay Prawns and finally to Duck. His numeracy was rather more advanced than his literacy and he tracked down page 151 without too much difficulty.

He then put his forefinger under each word and laboriously spelled it out, as he had been taught in Primary School.

'Ch-ch-oo-se a y-you-young b-ird w-ith s-o-ft p-l-i – pli – plibble? – never heard of it, what's it on about? – plibble f-eet.' The feet and the b-ill should be y-ell-ow. Yellow? What's it mean, bill? Beak? He looked dubiously at the birds. They were lacking in both feet and beaks. He felt certain that this was as things should be. 'It's only fish that gets cooked with their 'eads on,' he told himself. 'This book is crap.'

169

Nevertheless he persevered. While not aiming at the most succulent birds in the world, he wished to avoid either incinerating them, or undercooking. (He had heard plenty about salmonella from his mother.)

'A y-oung duck-ling does not require st-uff-ing, but it is usual to stuff an ol-der bird with s-age and onion stuffing at the tail. What tail? Don't matter, anyhow. And 'ow'm I supposed to know 'ow old it is? O-ven temp-er-a-ture fair-ly hot 400 or mark 5.'

He glanced at the cooker. As luck would have it he had set it at 400, but the red light was still showing, indicating that it had not yet reached the required temperature. Daisy now had the biscuit tin out, and was picking out the chocolate ones and doling them on to two plates.

'One for me and one for oo, one for me an' annunner for oo.'

Max decided to take a look round. As far as he could tell the house was deserted. He cautiously opened the door into the hall. The sound of television came from the sitting-room. He peered round the door. In one chair sat an old gentleman, with his eyes closed, apparently asleep. Max dimly remembered him as someone who had been generally around, but with a much lower profile than Grandma.

A glance about the room established that there was plenty of silver and a plethora of knick-knacks. Max was no authority on antiques, but most of these looked old to him.

'Could be worth a bob or two. Could be worth thousands.'

Max did not really mean to stay at Unicorn House and be reformed by Mrs Bagthorpe. This struck him as a terrible idea. For one thing, he did not like the Bagthorpes, and never had. The idea of waiting on them hand and foot had, if anything, less appeal than the prospect of a spell in jug. At least there you could lie on your bunk in your cell without anyone bothering you. At least you got three square meals a day without any aggro with beakless ducks. He was prepared to take a chance.

170

'If I get caught, I can just ask for it to be taken into consideration,' he told himself. 'In for a penny in for a pound. Might as well be hung for a sheep as a lamb.'

After a swift check on Grandpa he moved over to the fireplace. He lifted two satisfyingly heavy silver photo frames and put them in one pocket. He then hesitated before choosing a small Staffordshire figure to go in the other pocket.

'If I want any more, I'll 'ave to fetch a carrier.'

This seemed a good idea. There seemed no point in doing things by halves.

'Good afternoon,' said a voice. 'I don't believe we have met?'

Max whipped round, puny fists raised. Grandpa was regarding him with bright-blue eyes. The old codger had not been asleep at all.

'May I ask you who you are, and what you are doing?'

'Max. Max Fosdyke,' he stammered.

'Ah. How do you do?' Grandpa's manners were impeccable.

'I – I was just going to do a bit of cleaning.'

'It looked to me as if you were stealing,' said Grandpa mildly.

This observation left Max gobsmacked. He did not know what to say or do – he was in a play without a script. The whole scenario was beyond him. He had a vague idea that he should hit Grandpa over the head with a poker, then run for it. He was reluctant to do this.

'So what?' he said.

'I merely wondered why?'

'Skint, ain't I? Broke.'

'Ah.' Grandpa regarded him with those unnervingly clear eyes. 'I have a friend who is – as you say, broke.'

'Oh yeah?'

'A Mr O'Toole. I believe he is – broke – on a more or less permanent basis.'

' 'Ard cheese, then,' said Max.

'But I do not believe he ever steals. He makes extensive use of the Salvation Army.'

'You what? No fear! You won't catch me with that bunch of winos!'

'I believe they serve excellent soup. They also have television, he tells me.'

'Big deal.'

'You look rather young,' Grandpa observed.

'What d'yer mean?'

'To be embarking on a life of crime. Is that really what you want?'

Max hesitated. Put like that, he supposed it wasn't, not really. He had already had a taste of life on the run, and had not found it pleasant.

'Don't s'pose so,' he mumbled.

'You were always such a good little boy, I always thought.'

Max stared. Had the old geyser really noticed him, all those years ago? And thought him good? He could not but be pleased.

'Always hiding, I seem to remember. I had the impression you did not really wish to be here.'

'I din't. 'Ated it, I did. I told Ma I'd be all right on my own at 'ome, but oh no, 'ad to drag me 'ere, din't she?'

'I expect she was only doing her best as a mother,' Grandpa said. 'An excellent woman, Mrs Fosdyke, excellent.'

Max actually found himself quite proud of her.

'She deserves a good son, as I'm sure you are.'

Max hung his head. He fished in his right-hand pocket and put one of the silver frames back on the shelf.

'And obviously the problem is for you to find gainful employment. Only then can you hold your head high.'

Max held his head high and replaced the other frame.

'I wonder – have you ever considered becoming a private detective?'

Max boggled.

'Because, if so, I have a little matter I could put into your hands.'

'Private Eye!' exclaimed Max. He liked the sound of it.

'I would pay expenses in advance, of course, to enable you to carry out your inquiries.'

By now Max had replaced the Staffordshire figure, too. He was beginning to feel a certain excitement, an eagerness that he seemed to have mislaid years ago.

'Could be just the job for me!'

It certainly beat cooking beakless ducks hands down.

'I'm sure it could. What do you say?'

Max did not even hesitate.

'Done!' he said. 'You're on! Max Fosdyke – Private Eye!'

Fourteen

Max had been right in believing the house deserted. The entire family was out in the garden. They were out there for the kill – or, rather, looking for Aunt Celia.

When Mr Bagthorpe spilled the beans about the Phantom Twins and the Green-Eyed Angel, Uncle Parker genuinely felt like murdering him.

'Twins!' cried Grandma. 'I must double up my order for black wool!'

'Phantom Twins, Mother,' Mr Bagthorpe told her. 'Bet you've never had them before,' he said to the *Sludge* men. 'All the other stuff's been done to death – all those multiple births and infra-red fertilization and grandmothers giving birth! This is a brand-new angle.'

The *Sludge* men thought it probably was.

'Apart from anything else, it'll be an immaculate conception by definition,' he continued. 'You could tie that in with the Angel.'

'Er – where is Mrs Parker now?' asked Tony Wyman.

'Is this true, Russell?' Mrs Bagthorpe realized that here, under her own nose, was a Problem she had never yet encountered in her years as Stella Bright.

'Of course it's true,' her husband told her. 'You know Celia.'

'What's going on?' It was Rosie, closely followed by Tess and William. They could scent a good row a mile off.

174

'Your Aunt Celia's expecting twins,' Mrs Bagthorpe said.

'How many times do I have to tell you – '

'Twins!'

'Holy Moses!'

'Scylla and Charybdis!'

'Jekyll and Hyde!'

'Romulus and Remus!'

'You're joking!'

Mr Bagthorpe caught sight of the rapidly retreating figure of his brother-in-law.

'After him!' he shouted. 'She's out there somewhere with Daisy!'

Here he was only half right. Daisy and Arry Awk were busy in the kitchen.

A hue and cry was on. They all streamed into the garden and kicked up such a hullabaloo that the *Sludge* men in the outhouse wasted further valuable oxygen crying for help.

'Come on, Zero,' Jack said. 'If we find Aunt Celia first, we'll tell her to hide.'

He did not believe that she deserved to be hounded by the *Sludge*, and thought his father a rat for betraying her secret.

Aunt Celia was, of course, albeit unintentionally, already concealed. She was where her daughter had put her – in the potting-shed.

At first, she had been merely surprised at finding herself in there. She believed that Daisy was playing some kind of game, though she was at a loss to understand what her own part in this was meant to be. Aunt Celia was not very strong on games. She could not seem to get the hang of them. Even I-spy was beyond her. She could not be brought to see that the things spied must be in actual view, rather than in her own mind's eye. She would choose the letter m, and then when 'mirror,' 'mantelpiece', 'magazine' and so on had been exhausted, the answer would turn out to be 'mermaid'. She could never understand the

175

indignation that followed. She could see the mermaid quite clearly, she said, right down to the greenish-gold scales and ivory comb.

Hide and Seek was equally hopeless. She could hide, all right; it was when she was the seeker that trouble set in. She would become distracted by noticing the way the light struck a windowpane, or by seeing a petal fall from a rose, then go off and write a poem about it, leaving everyone else concealed in awkward places, half stifled or getting cramp. Games such as Pass the Parcel and Musical Chairs Uncle Parker would not allow her to play at all, for fear of overexcitement which, in her case, could easily lead on to full-blown hysteria.

Three people had now been imprisoned in the potting-shed that day, and in each case the victim's reaction was different. In Aunt Celia's case, it was at first merely a heightened sense of bewilderment which was her customary response to the real world. Half her life was spent wondering where she was, and why. The fact that she knew the answers to these questions the rest of the time was entirely down to Uncle Parker.

The Knoll was not so much a home as a protected environment for the last of a rare (and, in this case, threatened) species. There, Aunt Celia was in her natural element. All was harmonious to the eye, sweet music usually drifted through the air, there was no discordant note, nothing to jar.

The potting-shed was in rude contrast to all this. It had not been much to write home about even before Billy Goat Gruff had had a go at it. No one had thought of introducing a colour scheme. The walls were hung with scythes and rakes rather than paintings. The floor was strewn with soil and smashed flower-pots rather than oriental rugs.

Aunt Celia's huge eyes travelled over this unprepossessing scene in bewilderment. Who could possibly live here?

'Oh poor, poor souls,' she murmured.

Vague memories stirred of the fairy-tales, of poor woodcutters who lived in miserable huts in the forest. This must be one such place. (There would have been no use in pointing out to her that fairy-tales took place – if at all – long ago, and that this was the twentieth century. Uncle Parker took care to ensure that his wife never saw a newspaper, or television. He told people, in a garbled quote from Blake, that she lived in her own world, of which this vegetable world was but a pale shadow. She knew nothing of ram-raiding or gerrymandering, fluoride or the Welfare State, let alone how to boil an egg.)

Tears of pity rolled down Aunt Celia's cheeks. She began to wonder how she could help. Most people would have seized the broom that stood propped by the door and set about clearing up. Aunt Celia's instinct was to decorate. In a single graceful movement she dropped to the floor. (Had she had to do her own washing, she might have thought twice about this.) As she did so, she made out certain primitive signs and symbols drawn in the dust.

'Primeval . . .' she murmured. 'The beginnings of time . . .'

These were in fact the abortive games of Noughts and Crosses played earlier by Grandma and Max. She gazed at them in awe, then, with a long white forefinger, began to make her own drawings.

The posse in the garden at first drew blank. Uncle Parker raced on ahead. No one had seen him move this fast before – he went in for a laid-back, dawdling saunter (though Jack had some-times got up early enough to see him jogging). The rest streamed after him like the string of characters in *Henny Penny*, with Grandma bringing up the rear.

'Celia!' called Uncle Parker. 'Celia!'

Eventually he made for the Dead Sea. He well knew that his wife would not go there voluntarily, but she had been with Daisy, for whom the place seemed to exert a morbid attraction.

It was when they all reached it and stood round puffing and

177

blowing, that the *Sludge* men realized that they were in some new dimension. They gaped at the curdled water and its bloated occupants. They cringed at the sight of the fish Daisy had scooped out earlier. This was pollution on a scale beyond anything they had so far witnessed.

'Get some pictures of it!'

Mr Bagthorpe was triumphant. Once these hit the national headlines, compensation was in the bag. It might even bring Greenpeace down on Daisy Parker. The RSPCA could step in.

'Not here, then,' said Tony Wyman to Uncle Parker. Then, with unconscious reference to Uncle Parker's earlier fib, 'What price Ophelia, eh?'

Uncle Parker did not even hear him. He sped off, followed by the younger Bagthorpes, to whom the fate of the goldfish was old history.

The *Sludge* men made notes and took photographs, and tried to get some kind of picture of what had happened.

'Chemical spillage? In a private garden?'

'Nothing of the kind,' said Mrs Bagthorpe, who was herself a member of Greenpeace.

'Not *experiments*?' The reporter could hardly imagine for what purpose. Certainly not for cosmetics, or anything to do with health.

'Certainly it was an experiment,' Grandma said. 'Darling Daisy is a natural experimenter.'

'Experiment my foot,' said Mr Bagthorpe. He went on to fill in the reporter. He doubled the quantities of everything involved. 'Jack took away three barrowloads of empties,' he claimed. 'There were over a hundred rare fish in there – worth thousands.'

'Where is this child?' asked the reporter.

'God knows. Can you *believe* this?' he spread his hands, indicating the blighted pool.

The reporter admitted that he could not.

178

'And you say the goat is hers?'

'You saw what it was doing to my study. Get some pictures. Write it down.'

'We'll do it later. When we've interviewed Mrs Parker.' He looked about him. 'Which way did they go?'

The *Sludge* men set off with some urgency. Judging by what they had seen so far, murder was still on the cards.

Mr Bagthorpe and his wife, neither of whom was very fit, had done enough running for one day, and followed at a fast walk. Grandma opted to make her own private search.

'I am more concerned about Daisy than Celia,' she said. 'If she is out here, I shall find her. We have a natural affinity that will draw me to her.'

Mr Bagthorpe let that one go.

It was Jack who suggested the potting-shed. The goat, Max and Grandma had already been shut in there by Daisy, but overkill was her second name.

Uncle Parker flung open the door and there she was. She was crouched in a foetal position against the wall under the window. Her face was streaked with grime and tears, her eyes were wide and blank. Her fairy-tale had turned to nightmare.

It was only much later that they learned about the spider. Aunt Celia was in such deep shock that she did not speak for three days. She had a lot of phobias, ranging from snakes to red geraniums, but spiders were top of the list.

When she saw this one, scuttling among the shards of plant pots she was arranging, she screamed. Aunt Celia had a very healthy scream for one so fragile. Mr Bagthorpe said it could shatter plate glass at a hundred yards. She screamed . . . and screamed . . . and screamed.

When Aunt Celia screamed, Uncle Parker, as a rule, came running. He dropped whatever he was doing and ran. Often he reached her before she had opened her mouth for the second scream.

179

On this occasion, nothing happened. No one heard. Quite apart from the racket going on inside the house, the potting-shed was in a remote part of the garden, among the vegetables.

Aunt Celia was completely thrown by this. To begin with, she screamed as a natural reaction to seeing a spider, and knowing that she was shut up with it (and hundreds more) in a confined space. But when she realized that nobody was coming, she began to scream in earnest. And now she was screaming not only because of the spider, but because of a huge, over-whelming sense of abandonment and isolation. She was screaming at a deaf, indifferent universe.

She screamed for a considerable length of time. She did not speak for three days afterwards, not only because she was in shock, but because her voice had given out. It was at the point when she was trying to scream but nothing was coming out that she curled up and tried to crawl back into the womb.

When the door of the shed opened to reveal Aunt Celia, the photographer instantly poised his camera for action, but Uncle Parker turned and with one smooth swing made to knock it out of his hands. He failed only because, as a *Sludge* man, the photographer was well used to this kind of tactic. The younger Bagthorpes peered past him to see the collapsed figure of their aunt, and were impressed by her uncanny immobility. They were as close as they ever came to being awestruck.

Uncle Parker moved swiftly forward and knelt beside her, heedless of his natty suit.

'Celia? Celia, dearest . . .'

She turned her head at the familiar voice but gave no sign of recognition. Uncle Parker did not mess about. He half guessed what had happened. Pausing only to make a swift mental note to murder his own daughter, he lifted Aunt Celia in his arms and carried her out. The *Sludge* men hurried after them, one clicking away, the other calling, 'What about my interview?'

He was keener than ever to get this. If such things as

180

Phantom Twins existed, Aunt Celia looked exactly as you would expect the mother of such phenomena to look.

As the procession hastened back towards the house it met up with Mr and Mrs Bagthorpe, who joined it, the former yelling, '*Now* what, for God's sake!' and the latter crying, 'Oh – surely not a miscarriage! Oh, how dreadful!'

'*Can* you miscarry Phantom Twins?' Tess asked.

No one knew.

'*She* probably could,' William observed.

'Look – he's putting her in the car!' Jack pointed.

Mr Bagthorpe was enraged.

'Stop him!' he yelled. 'He's clearing off! It's his daughter and his goat! Stop him!

No one did. Uncle Parker hopped into his car, started it up, executed a smart U-turn and roared off down the drive in a spray of gravel.

Mr Bagthorpe gave a howl of rage. He ran to his study window and looked in.

'That bloody goat's still in there!'

Jack peered past him.

'Looks as if he's asleep.'

This was not necessarily good news. The goat tended to doze after he had a meal. When hungry, he ate a lot of paper, and Mr Bagthorpe's latest scripts were in there.

Mrs Bagthorpe hurried inside, followed by the others. The hall was filled with thin, acrid smoke, and there was a strong smell of something unidentifiable, but probably burning. She uttered a low cry and pushed the half-open kitchen door.

'The oven!' yelled William, 'Some fool's left the oven on!'

Jack ran forward and turned it off, then opened the door. A cloud of smoke poured out. In there, incinerated in their foil dishes, were the remains of the Italian takeaway. The Bagthorpes stood there, choking and eyes stinging. Mrs Bagthorpe alone thought she knew what had happened. If her guess was correct, Max had got off to a very bad start as a cook.

'It is my fault,' she thought characteristically. 'I should have warned Max they were in there. He did exactly the right thing in turning the oven on high for the ducks.'

Her eyes watering, she turned them towards the table.

'They've gone!' she gasped.

'The ducks!' exclaimed Tess. 'They were on the table. They . . .' her voice trailed off.

The conclusion seemed inevitable. History was repeating itself.

'I think we can work *that* one out,' said Mr Bagthorpe grimly. He turned to the newsmen, coughing and blinking with the rest.

'*Now* you've got a story!' he told them. 'Show 'em, Jack!'

'*I'll* show 'em!' said William. 'Come on, everyone – Highgate Cemetery!'

Sure enough, a double funeral was in progress, with Grandma as chief mourner. The ducks were already lying in their shallow graves and Daisy was spooning earth over them, rather than orange sauce.

'Poor lickle dead ducks,' she was saying. 'Now dey can't dabble up tails all.'

The two men from the *Sludge* were trying to take things in. They looked in bewilderment at the assorted headstones of previous funerals.

'I can't get my head round this,' Tony Wyman whispered.

Daisy was so preoccupied that she did not even notice them, and Grandma put a warning finger to her lips.

'You must compose a lovely epitaph for them, Daisy,' she told her protégée. ' "Luck" rhymes with "duck", and "muck" and "suck".'

'Duckys duckys poor dead duckys,' Daisy intoned as she wielded her spoon.

'I'll wring her neck!' William glowered at what should have been his supper.

'You shut *up*!' whispered Rosie. 'Look – she's crying!'

Sure enough, tears were splashing down Daisy's cheeks. Her sincerity was not in doubt.

'Der!' she said, the corpses thinly covered. 'Now we dot to sing a hymn.'

She straightened up and saw the others. Her face, smudged with dirt and tears, broke into a radiant smile.

'Now *lots* of people can sing der hymn,' she announced.

Her optimism was short-lived.

'She's got a hope! said William bitterly. 'Go on – take some pictures. Write it down. She should've been put down at birth.'

'I have no objection to being photographed,' said Grandma, as if that would have made any difference. The photographer was clicking away, getting shots of everyone present, and as many headstones as he could.

'You gotter sing oo gotter sing!' screamed Daisy. 'It's not finished!'

'*You* will be,' William told her, 'when this gets out.'

'There's not a playschool in England'll take you!' added Tess.

Daisy had already been suspended from her playgroup following a fire in the sandpit. Uncle Parker had been making approaches to several others, but with little success. News travels fast in nursery circles. As it happened, Daisy cared not a fig. She had thought playgroup very dull, with its sandpit and building bricks and Wendy house. She was also scornful of her fellow-playmates.

'Dey jus' silly,' she told everyone. 'I like Arry Awk best.'

It later emerged that it had been Arry Awk's idea to bury the ducks.

The *Sludge* men and the younger Bagthorpes made their way back to the house, the latter gloomily contemplating a duckless supper.

'The thing is,' Tony Wyman told them, 'we still haven't tracked down the others.'

183

'What others?' asked William.

'Ken and Bill. Apparently they came here earlier.'

William kept quiet. He naturally assumed that these were the pressmen he had earlier sent to The Knoll, whereas the missing men were the ones Uncle Parker had directed to Unicorn House.

'Any ideas?' Tony asked.

'Better go and have a good prod round in the Dead Sea,' William told him. 'For all we know, Daisy's into Burial at Sea.'

Nobody else bothered to make any suggestions. Nobody cared what had happened to the missing *Sludge* men. What was on their minds was their missing supper. It was therefore in unaccustomed silence that the group approached the house.

It so happened that the missing men were just about to make another bid for freedom. One of them felt sure he had heard a familiar voice during all the *brouhaha* about the goat.

'It was Tony Wyman, I tell you,' he said. 'They'll have sent him after us.'

'Is it still today?' asked Ken.

They were by now thoroughly disorientated. They were beginning to think they could smell a decomposing body, though neither mentioned this. Each could picture the moment when the door was finally opened and there were *three* decomposing bodies.

'I think we should risk another try,' Bill said. 'I think oxygen must be getting in here, somehow. It'll be getting in through the keyhole.'

'In that case, I'll have a fag,' said Ken, feeling for his packet. He had already finished the boiled sweets. 'Hey – that's it!'

'What?'

'My lighter! We can look in that freezer!'

The minute he had said it he realized that he did not *want* to look in the freezer. Nor, evidently, did his companion.

'Put it away,' Bill told him. 'Thought you'd quit smoking.'

'You always get a last smoke before they hang you,' Ken

184

said. 'Or shoot you. I'm under a lot of stress here.'

'Tell you what,' Bill said. 'We'll have one more go. Then we'll *both* have a smoke.'

'But you've never – '

'I'll take it up,' said Bill grimly. 'Never too late.'

'You kick, I'll hammer and we'll both yell. Right?'

They began to kick and hammer and yell with all the desperation of condemned men. This time they were heard.

'Sounds as if the goat's off again,' remarked William.

'That's not the goat,' said Jack. 'Someone's yelling.'

Sounds like "Help",' Tess said. 'Well, that just about sums it up. We all need help.'

The pressmen knew at once who it was.

'Come on!' They raced towards the house and came to a halt by a door that by now would have been off its hinges, had the house not been built when they knew how to build houses.

At first, the rescuers could not make their own voices heard above the racket.

'Bill!' yelled Tony. 'Ken!' He seized the handle. It's locked!'

'Who're Bill and Ken?' asked Rosie.

'Search me,' said William. 'But no prizes for guessing who shut 'em in there.'

'Oh you *would* say that!'

'*Bill*!' bellowed the reporter, and he delivered a mighty kick at the quaking door.

Silence.

'Bill? Ken? You in there?'

There followed the sound of grown men sobbing.

'Let us out, let us out!'

'Door's locked.' Tony turned to the interested spectators. 'Where's the key?'

William shrugged.

'It's usually in there,' Jack told them. 'I don't think there is a spare.'

'Get a grip on yourself, Bill,' Tony told his colleague. 'No – listen – who shut you in there?'

'It was a kid,' the muffled voice sobbed. 'A little kid!'

'With a goat!' came a croak. Ken's voice was evidently going the same way as Aunt Celia's.

'Told you!' William was triumphant.

It so happened that Daisy and Grandma were now approaching, the funeral over. Jack raced to meet them.

'Daisy! Those men you shut in the outhouse. Where's the key?'

'Dey bad men and dot to stop in prison and be sorry,' Daisy informed him.

'Yes, I know – but where's the key?'

'Lock der door and *frow* away der key!' Daisy chanted.

'Where? Where'd you throw it?'

She beamed.

'I finked ever so hard and I frowed it *hard* as I can!' She demonstrated the throw.

'But *where*?'

'Splash!' cried Daisy.

Jack stared, horrified.

'An den I dot annunner key and frowed it – splosh!'

The keys to both the study and the outhouse were at the bottom of the Dead Sea.

Soon after this discovery things snowballed to an extent that almost begs description.

Needless to say, no one volunteered to dive into the Dead Sea to recover the missing keys (though Mr Bagthorpe did suggest that Daisy should be lowered down to do this).

'I forbid anyone to go in!' said Mrs Bagthorpe unnecessarily. 'It is a health risk.'

To this Mr Bagthorpe replied that Daisy was a health risk, and asked the whereabouts of a spare key to his study. This had been pocketed so often, and by so many people, after Daisy's first foray in there, that nobody knew. His first instinct was to break down the door, but he realized that this, though probably satisfying at the time, would be counter-productive. His survival depended on his being able to go in there and slam the door on the rest of the world. He stomped off to find a locksmith in the Yellow Pages.

Mrs Bagthorpe began to comb the house for the missing Max, unaware that he had embarked on a career as Private Eye, and was at this moment boarding a bus for Aysham, where he hoped to track down the huge, bearded man described by Grandpa.

Here he was to be unlucky. At the Crown and Mitre the receptionist had noted the absence of Mr Bagthorpe's car. After an hour, she called the manager.

'Could just be a runner,' he said, meaning the kind of person who runs off without paying his bill.

'But he hadn't stayed the night,' she objected. 'He hadn't had a free breakfast.'

This was true. In the manager's experience, such people did as a rule make use of the hotel's amenities before doing a runner.

'So what's he been doing up there?' he wondered.

There was only one way to find out. He took the receptionist with him as witness, and she took a master key and the copper warming-pan.

Things would not have been so bad if the tramp had already drunk enough Scotch to put him out, and if he had not had an unmistakable Irish accent. As it was, the pair, after the first hideous encounter, fled. Back in reception Dilys's hands were shaking too much to tap out 999 and the manager had to do it for her. He then made the bold move of evacuating the hotel. The only way he could do this was by setting off the fire alarm, wired in to the local fire station. The chaos that followed was so extreme that it was a pity Mr Bagthorpe was not there to see it. It more than paid off his grudge against the hotel trade and its pleated loo rolls.

The Emergency Services, lights and sirens going, swooped down on the Crown and Mitre, with a posse of press cars in hot pursuit. Their long vigil outside the police station was paying off. When, minutes later, two squad cars roared out of Aysham in the direction of Passingham, half the press went after them.

Max, sitting upstairs on the bus and enjoying his first fag in ages, noted the procession speeding in the opposite direction, headed by flashing blue lights, and congratulated himself on his career move.

So it was that when Tony Wyman, distraught and disorientated as ever a *Sludge* reporter gets to be, finally took a sledgehammer to the potting-shed door, the nation's press were there *en masse* to record the moment.

It was a bad day for the *Sludge*. When the shaming picture of two of its leading newshounds, cowering and tearful, appeared on the front pages of every newspaper but his own, the editor offered his resignation. It was accepted. It was not so much the humiliation of the imprisonment, but the revelation of how it had happened. Pictures were published of Daisy Parker, showing her at her most wide-eyed and innocent and cuddling a docile Billy Goat Gruff, rather in the manner of Titania and the translated Bottom. Both Bill and Ken had to emigrate to Australia, no UK tabloid being prepared to take them on.

The Bagthorpes themselves moved fast when the police and press cars came screaming up the drive.

'Shut the doors!' yelled Mr Bagthorpe. 'Batten down the hatches! It's a siege!'